MW01141553

WHERE LOVE WENT

LINDSAY DETWILER

Sequel to **Then Comes Love**

HOT TREE
PUBLISHING

Where Love Went © 2016 by Lindsay Detwiler

Where Love Went is a work of fiction. All names, characters, events and places found therein are either from the author's imagination or used fictitiously. Any similarity to persons alive or dead, actual events, locations, or organizations is entirely coincidental and not intended by the author.

For information, contact the publisher, Hot Tree Publishing.

www.hottreepublishing.com

Editing: Hot Tree Editing

Cover Designer: Claire Smith

Format: RMGraphX

ISBN-10: 1-925448-22-3

ISBN-13: 978-1-925448-22-1

10 9 8 7 6 5 4 3 2 1

Dedication

To my mom,

my shopping buddy, biggest fan,

and best friend

Prologue

Her bright yellow luggage, complete with a lucky rabbit's foot, sat precariously stacked by the door. Her passport was ready, her favorite fanny pack was within reach, and her traveler's guide also sat nearby. Everything was ready for Charlotte's moment in paradise, her check off the bucket list. She was ready to make the memories she hadn't had a chance to, to take the honeymoon they hadn't.

It was hard for Charlotte to believe an entire year had gone by. One year of wedded bliss. Well, not exactly. There had been turmoil and strife. The difficulties of merging two lives together, especially two lives filled with 160 collective years of baggage, memories, and knick-knacks. Combining all their stuff into one apartment had been its own special challenge. Of course, there had also been the nursing home stint right before their wedding and the doctor's forbiddance of her going on a plane.

But there had been beautiful moments. Not just for Charlotte—Amelia and Annie had found their own grooves, their own places in the world of romance in the past year. As the seasons revolved around and a calendar year passed, all three women had solidified their places in a new love, a love never expected by any of them.

Annie and Amelia had been taking full advantage of their new lease on life. Both had traveled immensely in the past year and had experiences Charlotte could only dream about. But now, her time for dreaming was up. It was her turn to take life by the horns, to see some of the world she had been too busy for earlier in life. She was tired of Leonard talking about all of his travels and memories. Why couldn't her life be exciting, too? If it wasn't too late for love, it surely wasn't too late to cross some places off her bucket list.

So now, with their first wedding anniversary coming up, it was time for just that. She had finally planned the honeymoon of her dreams. Ireland with all of its fantastic sights awaited her and Leonard.

It had been a difficult sell.

"Ireland? Why would you want to go there? It's so rainy and miserable," Leonard had argued when she explained her grand plan.

"I've just always wanted to."

"Well, I suppose it could be worse. You could've said Alaska, I suppose." Leonard sighed. She'd winked at him, knowing she had won.

With that, they had visited the travel agent and planned their three-week Irish excursion.

Now they were in the final moments of preparations. Charlotte had a suitcase full of green and some four-leaf-clover scarves. They had made arrangements for everything from emergency medical services in Ireland to their mail. They were ready for some adventure, some excitement.

But there was just one small problem, one tiny kink in the plan.

They wouldn't get to go.

Chapter One

Charlotte

"Don't be ridiculous, Leonard. Of course I'm getting the door. What? You think a robber's going to waste his time at the old people's home?"

"Of course not, Charlotte. Get back in bed. Who would possibly be at the door at this hour other than a robber?" Leonard hissed at her, trying to yank her arm. He didn't have his glasses on, so he didn't even make contact with her.

Charlotte shook her head at the silly man.

"I'll take my chances," she whispered as he groaned and got out of bed.

"If we end up tied up it's because of you," he grumbled, rubbing sleep from his eyes. The pounding continued as

Charlotte grabbed her glasses from the nightstand on her way from the room.

"Coming," she yelled.

"Great, now the robber knows we're here." Leonard sighed, following closely behind.

"You've been watching too much *Dateline*." As she crossed the kitchen and put her hand on the doorknob, she begrudgingly paused. She couldn't admit Leonard was right. Peering at the clock on the stove, she realized it was 11:06 p.m. Probably not the smartest time to open your door. But she was committed now and couldn't admit she had the creeps, not with Leonard right there ready to say *told you so*. So Charlotte flung the door to the right, and waited to face her attacker.

The sight in front of her eyes in the darkened hallway was both glorious and terrifying.

Amelia stood in sweatpants and a hoodie, tears streaming down her face. Her hair was a frizzy mess and her eyes were bloodshot.

"Grandma, I'm so sorry. My flight just got in and I was going to wait to see you until tomorrow but I just needed to talk. Oh my gosh, you were sleeping. I'm an idiot."

Charlotte was horrified by the potential reason behind Amelia's sudden visit. She was supposed to be in Amsterdam right now. She wasn't due home until Thanksgiving.

"Don't be silly, dear. Come in, come in." She ushered the distraught girl—she would always be a girl to

5

Charlotte, even though she was in her thirties—into the kitchen, wrapping her arms around her once she was inside. Despite the potential circumstances, it felt so good to feel her granddaughter in her arms, to have her here. Video chatting wasn't the same, no matter what Amelia said.

After a long minute of Amelia snotting into Charlotte's pajama top, Charlotte pulled slightly away.

"Honey, what's wrong? What is it?"

She led them toward the kitchen table, pulling out a chair for her granddaughter. She caught Leonard's eye and nodded toward the scone cupboard. Leonard didn't need to be asked; he obliged her silent request, presenting the girl with some scones. She hungrily ate one before speaking.

"It's just, well, everything's such a mess, Grandma. I didn't know who to go to," she began. Charlotte wanted to scream, to prod the girl. She needed to know what was happening. Was it Owen? Was it the band? Was it the tour? What could possibly have Amelia this upset? Things were going so well for her. She and Owen were living their dreams, touring the world, climbing the charts. They were the talk of the town.

Charlotte fought the urge to speak, instead sitting silently, giving Amelia time and space to tell the story herself. Amelia's eyes spilled over and she swiped away the tears.

"Things are just so perfect. Owen and I were just talking a few weeks ago about how we couldn't imagine having a different life than what we have. Grandma, it's just… it's everything we both wanted. We're seeing the world, Owen's getting popular. I'm writing songs, Grandma, real songs. And people like them. I've got a song on the radio. *The radio.* Can you believe it?"

"I know, sweetie. It is all perfect. So why are you here? What's wrong?"

"It's just, I don't want to mess it all up. This is going to mess up everything." The tears were gushing now. Charlotte was so confused.

"What is, darling?" She reached for Amelia's hand, gently rubbing circles on the top of it.

"I'm pregnant."

Charlotte's heart stopped for a second. She thought maybe she was having another heart attack. But no, she wasn't. Her heart was stopping with joy. *A baby!* She was going to be a great-grandma. This was grand!

"Darling, that's wonderful news! I'm so happy for you," Charlotte cheered. But Amelia didn't reciprocate. And suddenly Charlotte put it together. This wasn't good news, not to Amelia at least.

"Grandma, no it isn't. This is changing everything."

"Well, yes. A baby does change everything. And I know it's scary. But it's going to be fine, Amelia. Is this it? Is this what you were so upset about?"

"You don't understand. It was just a few weeks ago when Owen and I were talking about us. And we were talking about how we didn't want to be the couple who settled down and bought a three-bedroom ranch house and a minivan. We both agreed we didn't want the whole wedding and baby thing. Not now, at least."

"Well, darling. Things change, right? I'm sure Owen's excited now, huh?"

"No."

"What do you mean?"

"Owen doesn't know."

"Well certainly you're planning on telling him?"

Amelia just looked up. "Yes. No. I don't know. Grandma, it's just a mess. This is going to change it all. His career, our life. It's going to change everything."

Charlotte patted her granddaughter's hand. "Honey, it's going to be fine. Owen loves you. And yes, you're going to have to reevaluate some things. But a baby, well, that's just beautiful. You're going to be wonderful parents."

Amelia shook her head. "I don't think Owen's going to be as excited as you think. His career is taking off. This is terrible timing. I don't think he's going to be happy at all. And I don't want to be the one who ruins his career. His life. I don't want to be that woman."

"Well, Amelia. I don't mean to be… well… forward. But did you, you know, think about this in the bedroom? Take some precautions?"

"Grandma, really? I'm thirty-four. I think I know how to prevent pregnancy. It wasn't planned."

"Of course. It was silly, really. Look, Amelia. I know you're upset. I know you think this is bad timing, and maybe it is. But a baby is a miracle. You'll be fine.

Really. You need to just talk to Owen about it. You need to figure it out together."

Amelia planted her forehead on her arms, curled up on the table. "I just need some time to think about everything. I don't want to just spring this on him. I want to figure out how I feel about it before I tell him."

"Well, yes, dear. I get that. So take some time. Is that why you came home? Did you come alone?"

Amelia nodded. "I told Owen I missed you and Mom. Which is of course true. I told him I wanted to take a few weeks break from the tour, do some relaxing. He seemed confused, but he understood. Touring is exhausting. I figured it would buy me some time to figure it all out."

"Amelia, I just don't know what there is to figure out. You love each other. You're having a baby with the man you love. So you're not married. So you're not exactly settled in one state right now. It'll be okay. You'll be okay," Charlotte reassured, meaning it. If anyone could navigate unconventional waters, it would be those two. They were the perfect metaphor for quirky love.

"I just… I don't want him to feel trapped. To feel like he has to be with me because of this. I vowed I would never do that to a man. And now I have."

"Amelia, I don't mean to intrude," Leonard offered. He had been silently eating his scone at the table the whole time. Charlotte glanced at him, a bit nervous about what would come out of his mouth. This was a difficult situation. She hoped he didn't make it worse.

"Owen loves you. That man is crazy about you. I see

it every time he looks at you. I don't think he would ever feel trapped. I think he wants to be trapped. Did you ever consider that maybe the reason he says he doesn't want to settle down and have kids is because he thinks that's what you want to hear? This might be the best news he's ever heard. You'll never know, though, if you don't tell him."

Amelia looked at her step-grandfather with a grin. "Thanks, Leonard."

"So what am I, chopped liver? I give you the same advice and you cry. He says it, and he's a hero?" Charlotte teased. Amelia finally gave her genuine smile.

"I knew coming here would be a good idea," she said, taking another scone.

They sat for a moment, basking in the heaviness of the news. "So what are you going to do?" Charlotte asked.

"I'm going to sit it out for a few weeks, take some time for me. And then I'll go from there. I mean hey, I have eight months, right?" Amelia joked, her hand instinctively going to her stomach.

Eight months, Charlotte thought as she eyed her luggage in the corner of the kitchen. If one night could change a lot, eight months could certainly change everything.

Chapter Two

Charlotte

"Don't you want to at least think about it?" Leonard whispered when they were back in their room. Charlotte had silently wheeled her yellow luggage back to the room. She didn't want Amelia to see it. This would be their secret. Amelia had enough to deal with; Charlotte didn't want guilt to play a role.

"Leonard, I *have* thought about it. Now my granddaughter is sleeping on our couch, tears staining her face. My great-grandbaby is on his or her way, and his or her daddy doesn't even know. My family needs me right now. Look, we have plenty of time. We can go next month. But I cannot leave Amelia right now. She needs me." Charlotte's back was propped against her pillow.

"You're right, honey," Leonard said, leaning in to kiss her cheek. "I was just looking forward to getting you to myself. I'm being selfish."

Charlotte turned to look at him. "Believe me, I was looking forward to it too. But I just won't enjoy myself knowing Amelia's having such a tough time. And Annie isn't due back from Arizona for a few days. I can't leave Amelia alone in this."

"I'll call Belinda tomorrow and cancel. I think we can get a partial refund."

Charlotte leaned against his shoulder. "I'm sorry, Leonard. Thank you for understanding."

"Of course I understand. Family always comes first." They slinked under the covers, both yawning. Leonard turned out the light and rolled over, holding Charlotte in his arms. She felt his warmth wrap around her and felt the ease of sleep floating into her veins. Her old bones weren't used to being up at this hour, and her head surged with sleep depravity. She closed her eyes, her mind floating away into the world between sleep and alertness. And then she heard it. The familiar sound, the sound she had heard once already.

Knock. Knock. Bang. Bang.

"Are you kidding me?" Leonard murmured as Charlotte groaned.

"Grandma?" Amelia called from the living room couch, sleep and confusion in her voice.

As Charlotte slowly made her way to the living room, the knocking ceased but a voice took its place. Muffled from the door, the voice said only one word. "Amelia?"

"Well, if it's a robber, they know your name." Charlotte coughed as Amelia eyed her warily. "Here we go again." She plodded to the door and swung it open for the second time during the night that didn't want to end.

***

"Mom, I'm so sorry. Did I wake you?" Annie spewed, a ridiculous glow on her face. Charlotte was exhausted, wanted to be cranky and sardonic. But she was so delighted and surprised for the second time that night, she just smiled.

"Of course not, darling. Leonard and I were just jamming to some amazing music and getting ready to get wasted." She yanked Annie inside, wrapping her arms around her. Annie hugged her and then pulled back.

"Amelia? What are you doing here?" Annie asked, confusion giving way to delight as she ran toward her daughter. A reunion of hugs was happening in the kitchen as Leonard sauntered out, flipping on a few more lights in the process. Behind Annie, Joe appeared, also reaching in to give hugs.

There were hugs and kisses, hellos and how are yous. There was a lot of confusion and countless questions circling. Charlotte's groggy brain couldn't really process it all.

"It's a long story, Mom. I'll explain later," Amelia said. "What are you doing here? I thought you guys were at the Grand Canyon until Monday?"

Joe and Annie gave each other a knowing look. "Well,

we were supposed to be. But then some things happened, and we couldn't wait to get home and share some news with you. We were planning on coming to see Mom first and then flying to Amsterdam to surprise you, Amelia. But since you're already here, we can tell you both at once." Annie was beaming, a look on her face that hadn't graced her countenance in a long time. Charlotte couldn't help but smile.

Everyone stared, waiting for the revelation they all knew was coming. Charlotte didn't want to be a downer, to ruin Annie's moment. But she knew already. They had all known this past year it was just a matter of when, not if. The glow between Joe and Annie was palpable from a state away. There was a connection, an ease that had spawned from their moving in together. The next step was just a natural progression in the state of their relationship.

Annie smiled before holding up her left hand. Charlotte and Amelia noted a detail that hadn't been there before.

"Mom, is that a tattoo?" Amelia squealed.

"I have a wedding ring on my finger, and you're more worried about me getting inked?" Annie beamed.

"Well, I just never thought you would. That's awesome."

"So does this mean…," Charlotte began, already knowing the answer but wanting to give Annie her moment of glory.

Annie vigorously nodded. "We went to Vegas. It was

spur of the moment. I hope you guys aren't mad you weren't there. It's just, well, we're so happy. We wanted to make it official," she spewed, holding up Joe's hand to show another matching ring tattooed on his finger. He was also gleaming with the typical newlywed glow.

"Did you guys get married by Elvis?" Amelia teased, her once tear-stained face looking so much happier now. Annie's good mood was contagious.

"Yeah, we did. But it was classy," Annie defended. Amelia rolled her eyes.

"If you say so. But Mom, I'm happy for you guys. Seriously. This is great news." At the mention of the word "happy," Amelia got a faraway look in her eye.

Annie and Amelia hugged. "Honey, what's wrong? Where's Owen? Why are you here alone?" Annie put away her happiness for a moment to worry about her daughter. Amelia eyed Charlotte as if to ask whether or not she should get into all of the details.

"Listen, why don't we talk about all this tomorrow? It's been a busy day, and I don't know about you guys, but these old geezers are ready for bed." Charlotte stepped in, pointing to herself and Leonard. Truthfully, she was exhausted, but this stalling was more for Amelia's sake. She thought the girl looked worn. She needed some time to think before getting Annie involved too.

"Yeah, Mom. We can talk tomorrow. I'm fine, really. Nothing to worry about. I just needed to come home, to be here. All this touring has been intense."

Annie eyed Charlotte with a questioning look, but

obviously decided to let it go. "Okay. We'll meet up tomorrow, maybe for lunch?"

"Sounds good. Now you two get out of here. You've got some celebrating to do," Amelia insisted.

Annie turned to Charlotte. "What time's your flight tomorrow, guys?"

Charlotte turned to Leonard, proceeding with caution. "Well, dear, we've talked about it and we're going to postpone."

"What flight?" Amelia jumped in.

"Nothing, dear. Just a little getaway we were planning." Charlotte didn't want this to become a huge drama. Amelia had enough to deal with.

"Mom, it wasn't a little trip. It was your honeymoon to Ireland. Didn't you tell Amelia? Why are you canceling?"

"Grandma, you're heading to Ireland tomorrow? Oh my God, and here I am interrupting. I'm so sorry. I shouldn't have come."

"Why did you come? Amelia, what's going on? And Mom, are you canceling because of Amelia? Is there something I need to know?"

Leonard and Joe stood back as the tension heightened amidst the three women. Voices started showing inflections of panic, and everyone started to think the worst. Charlotte's head was spinning in a cacophony of confusion. It was too late at night for this.

"Enough!" Charlotte shrieked.

Everyone froze, not used to her raising her voice—at least not at anyone besides Catherine.

"Listen, everything's fine. It's just, both of you are back in town, and Leonard and I don't want to leave at a time like this. It's not often we're all back at home at the same time these days. Ireland can wait. We can go anytime. Honestly. Now, I don't want to hear any nonsense about it being anyone's fault. This was our decision. I want to spend my time doing what matters the most to me, and right now, what matters the most is spending time with the both of you."

Amelia approached. "Grandma, I know why you're doing this. And you don't have to. Really. I'm fine."

"I know you are, honey."

"Why wouldn't Amelia be fine? What's going on?" Annie demanded, pleading with her eyes to be let in on the secret.

Amelia sighed. Charlotte groaned. Leonard looked at the clock, sleepiness evident in his eyes.

"I'm pregnant," Amelia revealed.

The secret was out. Ireland was out.

Everything was changing. Again.

Chapter Three

Amelia

A squawking bird outside of Amelia's window woke her up abruptly the next morning. When she rubbed away the sleep from her eyes, she realized the sun was brightly cascading into the room.

She turned to peek at the clock. It was 8:00 a.m. Rolling over, she haphazardly grabbed her phone from the nightstand. Three missed calls—one from Charlotte, one from Annie, and one from Owen. So much for some peace and quiet to think things through.

She tousled her hair with her hands, sliding out of the bed. She felt like crap. After the debacle last night, she was drained. Her mom, of course, had needed to hash out every detail of the situation last night. Sitting around the table for a second time with a second round of scones, she'd filled her mother in about the baby, Owen, and her fears.

Annie ran the gauntlet of emotions with Amelia. There were tears of joy about her soon-to-be grandma status. There were her comforting words about Owen. And there was understanding.

She had left Charlotte's with Annie and Joe around one in the morning. Poor Leonard had fallen asleep on his recliner by that point.

Now, she was home, in her apartment. She was alone, left to think about her life, about where she went from here.

It really shouldn't be a question. It was easy. She would tell Owen about the baby, he would be thrilled, and they would figure things out. She loved Owen and he loved her. She wanted kids. Sure, not right now, but hey, when did things ever go the way you planned?

In her heart, though, she knew there was potential for way more complicated scenarios. She knew this baby wasn't what either had planned. She recognized this could change everything. At a time when she and Owen were finally getting everything they ever wanted, how could this be thrown into the mix?

She slogged to the kitchen, searching for some Pop-Tarts and some water—too bad she didn't have any milk—when the door flew open. Her heart dropped as she whirled around.

In the doorway stood a stranger. A girl, twentysomething, with lavish red curls, skintight jeggings, and knee-high boots. The girl took in Amelia's clearly disheveled state, looking at her with shock.

"Amelia?" the girl asked. Amelia just stood, drinking in the sight, not even able to spew out questions of what the girl was doing there.

She squinted at her, knowing the familiar lines of her face, the eyes. She recognized the bone structure, felt like the hair was identifiable.

And then it hit her. She'd seen this girl before. This was the girl in Owen's wallet, the picture he carried with him.

This was Janie.

"Janie? What are you doing here?" Amelia offered, not paying attention to the fact she was meeting her baby's aunt and being pretty off-putting about it.

"Didn't Owen tell you?"

"Tell me what?"

"Oh my goodness, I just thought you knew. He told me I could stay here for the next few months. I'm doing my residency at Cooperstown and needed somewhere to stay. He said since you guys were touring and everything I could stay here for a few months until I figure some stuff out."

Amelia just blinked. "Oh. No, he didn't mention it."

"Um, wow. This is awkward. I'm really sorry. I didn't realize... I didn't know. Where's Owen?" Janie asked, words tumbling out a mile a minute.

"He's still in Amsterdam. I just wanted to take a break and come home for a few weeks. He probably just forgot about this whole thing. It's been nuts on tour," Amelia said, slinking toward Janie, arms crossed around her chest in an attempt to cover the fact she wasn't wearing a bra.

"Look, I can leave. Stay in a hotel or something for a few weeks," Janie offered, her perfectly painted lips grimacing.

Amelia smiled, shaking her head. "Don't be ridiculous. I'm sorry, you just caught me off guard. You can stay here, not a problem. It's just so good to finally meet you."

Janie smiled back, a full, genuine smile that told Amelia they could be friends.

"Thanks so much. I really appreciate it. I promise I'll stay out of your hair while I'm here."

Amelia shook her head. "Seriously, it's fine. Make yourself at home."

"I will. Thank you," she replied, setting down her bag. "Well, I'm going to grab a shower and maybe a few hours of sleep. Night shift is a killer… oh, oops. Probably shouldn't make that pun working in the Emergency Room, huh? Anyway, I'm off work until tomorrow night, so do you want to do lunch? My treat?"

Amelia knew Grandma and her mom would probably be waiting to go to lunch with her. But something about Janie invited her in. She couldn't help but trust the girl, couldn't help but want to say yes.

So she did.

***

"Shit, Amelia. I'm sorry. I meant to tell you, and then the dates got away from me. I feel awful," Owen said that night when he called her.

"It's fine, Owen. Really. Your sister's great. We're really hitting it off." Amelia tucked her toes under the comforter in their room as she leaned back against the pillows. Janie was graciously sleeping on the couch, insisting she would not take their room.

"Yeah, she is. I knew you two would hit it off. But I should have asked you about it. I'm sorry."

"Owen, it's fine. How are things in Amsterdam?" Amelia tried to hide how overwhelmed she was feeling, tried to act normal.

"It's great, babe. Living the dream. I miss you, of course. But God, it's great, isn't it? I can't imagine living life any other way. I'm so glad you're with me on this. I'm so glad you're not like most women who have to settle down right away. I'm glad we can be wild and free right now, huh?"

Amelia's heart sank. That was exactly what she didn't want to hear.

"Amelia?" he asked after a few moments of silence. Tears were welling, threatening to spill over.

"Yeah?"

"You okay? You seem distant. Everything okay at home?"

"Yeah, everything's great." She was a terrible liar. He

could probably sense it.

"You sure? Because you don't sound like yourself."

"No, I'm just tired. It's been crazy here."

"Maybe I should take a break from the tour, come home with you."

"No!" she answered too quickly. She tried to cover the tenseness in her voice. "I mean, no, I'm fine. You need to focus on the tour. I'll be back over there before you know it."

They exchanged some basic conversation, some genuine I love yous, and then they both hung up, vowing to be back with each other soon.

But for Amelia, the vows felt like empty promises. Because after their conversation, she was more certain than ever this baby would ruin everything Owen had planned.

Chapter Four

Amelia

"Morning. How'd you sleep?" Janie asked Amelia the next morning as Amelia trudged to the kitchen for another Pop-Tart.

"I slept well. I should be asking how you slept on that god-awful sofa. I really wish you would let me trade you."

Janie was already up, gulping down some cereal and watching the morning news.

"Stop. We talked about this. I'm just grateful to have a place to stay for free while I sort out everything. So not another word," Janie mumbled between crunches of sugary flakes.

Amelia grabbed her packet of brown sugar pastries and headed to the couch to join Janie.

"So how are things going at the hospital? Does it feel good to have on the official coat?" Amelia asked, making friendly conversation. She liked that it didn't feel forced with Janie. Janie was easy to talk to. The circumstances were odd—two strange women living together, one Owen's sister and one Owen's lover. But Amelia saw something familiar in Janie—a pizazz, a spunk. It was the same thing she loved about Owen. It was the same thing she saw in herself.

"Yeah, it's good. Not exactly what I had in mind. I applied to a hospital in California too but didn't get picked. I guess I just got caught up in dreaming big, you know? Maybe Owen's wanderlust has inspired me. I've just been thinking about getting out of this town, going somewhere bigger. So it was sort of a blow, but I'm learning to love it. Cooperstown is a good hospital. I think I could be happy here."

"It'll all work out," Amelia said. She crunched on her Pop-Tart as Janie continued.

"I don't know what'll happen once my residency is up. I sort of just want to get out, to travel. See things, you know? I guess I just never felt like I had roots anywhere after Mom and Dad died. So it's not like I feel tied down. I imagine it's different for you, with your family being here and all. Is it tough, you know, all of the traveling?"

Janie had no idea how hard she had hit Amelia with these statements. Amelia spoke wistfully. "Yes and no.

I mean, I love the traveling, the spontaneity of our life together. And not to be sappy, but Owen just is home for me. I never really feel lost or alone, even when we're in some foreign country. But there are times I miss our life here. There are times I miss the settled feeling of sleeping in the same bed every night."

Janie nodded. "Well, there's nothing that says you can't have both. My brother's crazy about you, Amelia. You've been so good for him. I've never heard him talk about anyone like he talks about you. I've been so anxious to meet you, to see the girl who's inspired him, the girl he raves about. Now that I've met you, I get it. You're perfect for him."

Amelia smiled. "You're sweet. Thanks. I've been excited to meet you too."

"Yeah, well, pretty sure you didn't plan on meeting me yesterday in your pajamas as I broke into your apartment, huh?"

"Uh, no. I planned on at least brushing my hair for our first meeting. But hey, it worked out. It's all good."

"Yeah, it is. I don't mean to be creepy or forward, but I like you a lot. I think it's going to be awesome having you in our family."

"Thanks. But Owen and I aren't talking about getting married or anything anytime soon."

Janie winked. "Okay. If you say so. But I'm telling you, I think that's exactly what Owen wants." Amelia eyed her curiously, wondering if she knew something she didn't. Amelia was scared of the word marriage, had pushed it outside of her realm of possibility for the past year. But now, this zany redhead eating cereal on her couch had made her stop and question herself.

And surprisingly, without even knowing it, she made Amelia feel better about everything happening, baby and all. Maybe she was being ridiculous. Maybe Grandma Charlotte was right; maybe Owen would be thrilled about this baby, maybe all this worrying was for nothing.

Maybe, just maybe, if she thought about it, it wasn't Owen who was upset about the baby. Maybe it wasn't Owen who would push her away, who would be devastated about the changes the baby would bring.

Maybe if she were honest, it was herself she was worried about.

***

"Amelia! Hey! There's our famous hometown hero. What are you doing back here? Don't tell me you need a job," Kristin exclaimed when Amelia walked into Book World later that afternoon. She had a few purchases to make. Now, however, coming here seemed like a bad idea. If she picked up her books here, everyone would know in 5.6 seconds. Maybe she would go on Amazon instead.

"Hey. Just was in town and thought I'd stop by. I miss you guys." Amelia approached the book table Kristin was in front of. She aimlessly rearranged some books, habit dictating her moves.

"We miss you too, Miss World Traveler. How's everything? How's the tour?"

"Good. Busy. Crazy. But good."

"Where's that hunk of a boyfriend of yours?"

"Amsterdam."

"You left him in the city of sin without you? Are you nuts?"

Amelia just smiled. "He's so damn tired from all the traveling, I doubt he has energy for some sin. I just needed to come home for a bit, take a break."

"Must be hard being famous," Kristin nudged. "Us peons wouldn't even begin to understand."

"You're not a peon."

"If you say so. But hey, while you're here, do you want to help at the latte machine? It's jammed again."

Amelia wanted to say no. But in a way, she wanted to say yes. She loved touring with Owen, loved their careers were simultaneously going somewhere. But some days, she craved the simple life she had once known here. The life where the most strenuous occurrence was a broken latte machine. A life that didn't require passports and plane rides, a life without the constant restlessness. She sometimes missed having her feet planted right here at Book World, watching the world revolve around her as she stood still.

***

"Come on, big fella," Amelia coaxed, tugging on the giant's leash. This was probably the worst idea she'd had all year.

She had called the Stinsons this morning, offering to come walk Henry. They, of course, jumped at the chance.

"Yes, come! We'll pay double. Henry's missed you," Mrs. Stinson had cheered into the phone. Amelia doubted it was true. Still, it was nice to get in touch with her old life, the simple life. Plus, she needed something to occupy her during the day so she didn't go insane. She wasn't used to having so much free time.

"Come on, you can do it," she encouraged the dog. It was useless. Henry, now fifty pounds heavier than when she last saw him, rested on the concrete, huffing and puffing. For a moment, she feared the dog would expire, a heart attack probably only one breath away. He certainly had let himself go over the past year.

Standing over Henry, she felt in her pocket for her phone. It was buzzing, so she answered, knowing Henry wasn't going anywhere for a while.

"Hey, honey, how are things?" Owen asked, sounding breathless himself.

"Good. Just catching up with Big Henry."

"Really?"

"Yeah, why not? I mean, I missed him. What're you doing? You sound out of breath."

"Just got off stage. Wanted to call and say I missed you. Everything okay?"

"Yeah, everything's good." She tried to inject some enthusiasm into her voice, but it was hard to muster. As much as she wanted things to be fine between them, she could feel herself building a wall, brick by brick. Owen didn't understand what was happening with her. Which, of course, wasn't fair of her to hold against him. It was her fault he didn't understand.

"How's Janie?"

"Awesome. I love her, Owen. She's great."

"I miss you."

"I miss you too."

"When are you coming back?"

"I don't know. A few weeks, maybe? I'm enjoying my time here, catching up with everything and everyone."

There was a long pause.

"Hope you're not enjoying it too much."

"Of course not, Owen. I miss you. I wish you were here too."

"Then I'll come."

She sighed. "Don't be silly. It's just a few weeks. We'll be back at it together in no time. I just needed a break."

"From me?" Hesitation rang loud and clear in his voice.

"No, of course not." She gritted her teeth, closing her eyes at the blatant lie.

"Okay. Amelia, look, I know things are crazy right now. But it'll settle down. It's going to be okay."

"I know."

"I love you."

"I love you, too. I'll talk to you later. Gotta go."

The phone clicked, and Amelia sighed, not because she believed him… but because she knew things just might not be as picture-perfect as he imagined.

***

After an hour of playing tug of war with Henry's leash, Amelia brought the dog back home, gave him a kiss on his floppy head, and headed back to the apartment.

On her kitchen table, Amelia found a note:

Gone out with a few friends to catch up. Be home later. Hope you had a good day!

Amelia found herself smiling, feeling Janie's eclectic energy through the words on the page. She liked the girl, she really did. From her go-get-it attitude to her kindness, Janie just exuded likability.

Amelia put her keys on the counter, flipping through some mail. She saw the newspaper on the counter and decided to do something out of character—read it. Sitting down with a cup of hot tea a few minutes later, she flipped through, feeling totally matronly and totally old. What was she doing? She really was out of sorts.

As she glanced at the pictures, though, her fingers aimlessly flipping the pages, she stopped cold on page D1.

Staring at her with twinkling eyes was none other than Neville. He was wrapped around a woman, drop-dead gorgeous and plump in all the right places. They radiated love, even through the faded newspaper ink. "Wedding Announcements," the headline read.

She found herself perusing the article, reading the when, where and how. Devouring the details, she felt a slight pitch in her stomach, a small stab. She couldn't deny the fact it hurt a bit to realize it was supposed to be her by his side. At one time, she'd wanted to be the

LINDSAY DETWILER

woman on his arm in this picture. She had imagined a life, a secure, safe, predictable life with him. A life involving her living in this town, raising a family, and growing old together.

She knew she had made the right choice leaving Neville. Once her heart fell for Owen, it wasn't the same. Her love for Neville wasn't equivocal to the raw passion she felt for Owen, the mind-bending love she experienced when he walked into the room or when his fingers grazed hers. Owen was it for her, the one and only. She loved her life with him.

But a small, tiny pang beckoned her to consider the harsh truth. If she hadn't fallen for Owen, if she had married Neville, she wouldn't be at this crazy crossroads now. This baby would be a welcome miracle, a reprieve from the boredom she would probably be feeling. Neville would welcome the child into his arms, his safe and predictable arms, and they would cradle the child in a blanket of security and certainty. She wouldn't feel guilty for introducing Neville to this facet of life because it was what Neville would have plotted out for them. It wouldn't have thrown a wrench in his life or plans.

It wasn't that she wanted to be with Neville or have his child. But she had to admit, things with him would have been much simpler, much more predictable.

As much as Owen widened her heart and horizons, he also scared her with the unpredictability. When they were just dating, it was okay. But now a child was being introduced to the mix, and Amelia was left wondering:

32

could unpredictability equate to father material? And would Owen want it to?

She had a lot to sort out over the next few months, she thought as she carefully folded the paper, stowing it away into a closet of the past.

Chapter Five

Annie

"Butternut!" Annie screamed as she turned from pouring cereal to swat away the cat skulking toward her bowl. "Honestly, this house drives me crazy."

Annie huffed as the cat went sliding off the counter. Ten seconds later, another cat jumped on the counter, only to be shoved away.

Stirring her cereal with her spoon, she felt him wrap his arms around her. Despite the chaos of the morning and her frustration, she couldn't help but smile. He did that to her.

"Morning, love," he whispered in her hair.

"Morning," she replied, abandoning her breakfast to

turn in his arms. Joe kissed her then, temporarily taking her away from the chaos of her five-cat household.

When their lips parted, she sighed. "Much better." Annie turned back to grab her cereal, smiling like a fool. And then, as she walked to the table, she tripped over Peter.

"Ugh!"

Joe just chuckled. "I thought you said you missed the cats while we were away?"

"Well, then I got home and remembered what pains in the asses they are," she shouted, huffing as she stomped to the table.

"Oh, stop. They've just missed us."

"Oh, please. I know Mrs. Carlton fed them ninety cat treats a day." Mrs. Carlton was the seventy-year-old cat hoarder down the street. She was Annie and Joe's cat sitter whenever they went out of town.

"You love them," Joe said as he opened the fridge to grab the milk.

"If you say so."

"What do you have going on today at work?"

"The Tillson wedding final details. We've got to sort some things out. I have ten e-mails from the bride's mother that have been sitting since last week. I figure I better meet with them today before the mother has a coronary."

Annie grinned. Dealing with semi-psychotic brides and mothers was not always the best part of her new job. However, she loved it. The thrill of it, the challenge of making everything come together in an impossible way. She was made for this job. It turned out it had been a blessing she'd been fired. She never thought she would be saying that last year when she was canned from her customer service job.

Of course, a year ago, so many things were different. Looking back, Annie realized how empty she'd been then, how lost.

There was the career, of course. She hadn't even realized how bored she was there... until she'd started this job.

More than her career though, there was the emptiness she felt after losing Dave. She'd thought her love life was over, that she'd never find another man. She'd believed she would live out her days alone, save for the five cats scampering around her house.

And then came Joe.

He had come into her life when she had given up on excitement, on happiness. He had snuck his way into her heart, into her life. Over the past year, he had not only laid claim to her heart. He had completely and utterly overthrown everything she thought about love.

With him, she now knew that what she had with Dave had never even come close to love. Dave's heart had been a bargaining chip he used to claim ownership of her. It was conditional, it was stiff, and it was forced.

Not with Joe.

Over the past year, she had experienced more love and life with Joe than she ever could have with Dave.

There were the trips to places she'd never been: Niagara Falls, Florida, and the Grand Canyon. There had been a couple's massage and late-night ice-cream dates. There had been exotic dinners and sightseeing in New York City. There had been weekends at the theater, concerts, and shopping outlets.

But, if she were being honest, the big trips and exotic locales weren't the dominant elements of her memories. What stood out to her the most from this past year were the small moments. The nights at home watching Netflix, cuddling on the couch. The daily morning kisses and falling asleep in his arms. The random walks in the park, the laughter, and the small gestures of love. There was the hot chocolate apology after their first argument, during which Joe simply brought her a cup from the same café they had gone to on their first date. There was the time Joe had rushed Peter to the vet because his cough was getting worse, and Joe knew Annie would be devastated if anything happened to him. There were the subs in the fridge on Mondays because they were Annie's most hectic day at work. The small things, the little moments, told Annie Joe was the one for her, that he wouldn't be like Dave.

The small moments added up to the one, big conclusion Annie had this past week—she could marry Joe and not worry about him leaving her. This time, marriage would be forever. Love would be forever.

On the plane ride home after their impromptu elopement, she had been tempted to get nervous, to fear the honeymoon stage would wear off. But now, sitting at the breakfast table with Joe, talking about their cats, work, and the normal, day-to-day living kind of stuff, she knew there was no reason to be afraid. There wouldn't be an end to the honeymoon stage—because they had never been *in* the honeymoon stage. From the moment Joe walked into her life, she had been in the real-life stage. The kind of stage where love usurps lust, where reality is welcome and not avoided. Where candlelit dinners take the backseat to takeout on the sofa. Where suits and ball gowns hang in the back of the closet and jeans and T-shirts take precedence. Joe and Annie had a love that would last because they had a simple, true, realistic kind of love.

And Annie couldn't be happier.

As they kissed good-bye one last time before heading to their jobs, Annie winked at Joe.

"Bye, husband. Love you."

"Love you back, wife. Always."

Always. Now that was a word Annie could handle.

***

After assuring Mrs. Tillson the mints in the favors would be the perfect pastel pink they required, the DJ would not be bald, and the main entrée would be gluten free, Annie headed over to Amelia's apartment. She was exhausted from the overbearing mother-of-the-bride's interrogation and panic attacks, but she couldn't go home without checking on Amelia. Plus, her excitement over the news couldn't make her stay away.

A baby. Amelia was having a baby.

This was the most electrifying thing that had happened to her yet.

True, there was Amelia's clear panic to consider. The girl had been a train wreck the other night. But Annie chalked it up to hormones. Amelia was just nervous. She just needed a few days to think things through, to breathe. Annie had called her a few times yesterday to be met with "I'm fine, Mom," and "Mom! Please let me breathe."

She'd given her almost a day to breathe. That was enough, right?

Annie dashed into Amelia's apartment, which was unlocked. At the sound of the door, Amelia turned her head from her TV show. Annie tried to ignore the grimace on Amelia's face at the sight of her.

"Mom, what are you doing? I told you I was fine on the phone yesterday."

Annie took a seat on the couch beside Amelia. "I know what you said, but I had to check on you. Are you feeling better about everything?" Annie resisted the urge to pat Amelia's tummy. Even though there wasn't yet evidence of her growing grandchild, just knowing he or she was in there was so darn enticing.

"I don't know. It's just a mess. This wasn't what we had planned. But listen, we can't talk about this right now anyway."

"Why not?"

"Janie's here."

"Owen's sister?"

"Yeah. Long story. But she's staying here until she sorts some stuff out. She's in the bathroom."

"Amelia, we have to talk about this. You can't keep this secret forever. When are you going to tell Owen?"

"Mom, honestly. Not now."

"She can't hear us. I'll whisper. Now come on, stop avoiding the question."

Amelia sighed, rubbing her forehead with her hand. "Mom, I don't know. This is just a mess. Owen's finally getting his dreams. He's finally on tour like he wanted, and now this happens. I'm just afraid this is going to mess everything up."

"Honey, he loves you. And yeah, this might not be what you had in mind right now. But it's a baby. You're having a baby. He will want to know."

"It's not that simple." Amelia anxiously glanced toward the bathroom door. Thankfully, it was still shut.

"Of course it's simple. You love each other. There's a baby. What else is there to work out?"

"A lot, Mom. Now can we just drop this? I don't want to argue."

"We're not arguing. You're just being crazy. What are you so afraid of?"

"Everything. Losing him. Or keeping him because of the baby. I'm afraid to be a mom. I'm not ready for this. He's not ready for this. I don't want to raise this baby alone, but I don't want him to stay out of obligation."

"Amelia, you're being ludicrous. He's crazy about

you. And having a baby doesn't mean you have to give up all your dreams. You can figure it out."

"Mom, you don't know what you're talking about."

"Really? You're right. I never had a baby. Oh wait," Annie teased, nudging Amelia. "Look, I know this complicates your plans. But Amelia, when you see that baby, when Owen sees that baby, everything is going to change. For the better. It's going to be messy and hectic and complicated, but it's also going to be wonderful. You'll see. Now don't keep Owen in the dark. You need to tell him. Sooner rather than later. Trust me."

"A baby?" a voice bellowed from the hallway. Annie and Amelia turned to see Janie, her mouth wide. "You and Owen are having a baby?"

Amelia glared at Annie before stomping back to her room. "Thanks a lot, Mom. Now you've really done it," she shouted over her shoulder before heading to her room and slamming her door like an insolent teenager.

Janie and Annie just stared at each other in mild horror. Annie crossed the room, thinking about going after Amelia, but deciding maybe she should actually respect Amelia's wishes to be alone this time.

So instead, she headed to Janie, now standing in the kitchen. "Hi, I'm Annie. Looks like we're going to be family soon."

Janie smiled, shaking off the surprise. "Yeah, looks like it."

Annie stood silently, appraising the girl, not sure what to do next. Mindlessly, she ambled over to Amelia's cupboards and pulled out a box of Pop-Tarts. She slid out a pack, took one of the pastries, and then slid it toward Janie, smiling.

"So, why don't you tell me about yourself while my daughter simmers down?" Annie asked, and Janie obliged.

Chapter Six

Annie

When she got home, there was a note on the kitchen table—which Arya was sitting on. *So much for keeping the cats off the counter and the table,* she thought before scooching the cat over to pick up the note. She'd officially given up.

Got called back to work for an emergency. Don't know when I'll be home. Love you.

"Looks like it's just me and the cats," Annie said to herself, still slightly off from the Amelia encounter.

After changing into sweatpants and a T-shirt, Annie decided to catch up on some soap operas she'd DVR'd. The Pop-Tart had appeased her appetite, at least for the time being, so she headed straight for the couch without a snack, to Butternut's chagrin. As she flipped on the television and started the first soap opera, she sighed. It felt amazing to be wrapped up in some fictional drama instead of the real-life drama she'd been dealing with.

Five minutes in, a kidnapping and a sultry kiss had already happened. Annie felt her head lolling, sleep creeping in.

But the dinging of the doorbell quickly snapped her back to reality. Maybe Amelia had had a change of heart and forgiven her for the misstep this afternoon. Quickly, she crossed her living room, five cats also running to greet the visitor.

Throwing open the door, Annie froze when she saw *him* standing there.

"Hi, Annie. Can I come in?"

"What the hell are you doing here?" The words tumbled out before she could stop them.

***

Five minutes later, she stared at the frozen face of the protagonist on her television as *he* sat beside her on the sofa, a cooing baby in his lap. *When you freeze the show, she has a double chin,* Annie found herself thinking. It was an odd thought to have, considering all the strange shit unfolding. But she couldn't bring her mind to deal with the man, the practical stranger, and the baby on her couch.

"Can I get you some water?" she finally asked when she averted her eyes from the television to him. It felt so weird offering her ex-husband a water in the house where he used to live.

It felt even weirder having her ex-husband sitting on her couch with a baby that wasn't hers.

"No, I'm okay," he practically choked as he carefully bounced the baby girl on his knee. He looked awkward as hell. The baby looked as uncomfortable as he did. She should probably offer to take her, her mothering instincts screaming.

But she couldn't. Her mind was in a state of disbelief, not allowing her to do anything. So she sat and waited for Dave to explain why he'd come, what he was doing in her house.

She had let him in only because he looked so dejected standing on her doorstep, baby in his arms, sadness in his eyes. "I didn't know where else to go," was all he'd said. It was all it took for her to crack open her door, to welcome in the ex-husband who had screwed her over.

It scared her how easy it was for him to worm his way back in.

Then again, what could she say? *Get out, take the baby and leave? We spent over a decade together in this very house, but now you can't even step foot in it?*

Yes, that's what she should have said. That's what she *could* have said. No one could blame her.

But damn, the guy was smart. He'd brought a baby with him. An innocent, adorable baby. He knew she wouldn't be able to push him out in the figurative cold with a baby in his arms.

A few more minutes passed, and the baby started crying. Dave looked like he was going to cry. So she took her from him, Dave passing her over willingly, his body practically going limp with relief when she was out of his arms.

"What's her name?" Annie asked, realizing how little she knew about Dave now. At one time, she'd been obsessed with knowing every horrifying detail about his new life. Now, she didn't even know his baby's name.

"Esmerelda."

Annie felt her face scrunch in horror, and then tried to cover it. "A fine, strong name," she bluffed.

"Melissa picked it."

"Enough said."

Annie rocked the baby gently, thinking how the hell she could shorten Esmerelda to anything less awful. Es? Esme? No, that was from *Twilight*. Elda? God, anything was better.

And then her thoughts were interrupted.

"She's gone."

Annie turned to him, baby still in her arms.

"What?"

"Melissa. She's gone."

Annie sat there. She wanted to ask questions, wanted to feel bad. But she felt… nothing.

"Where?"

He shrugged. "I don't know. I just came home yesterday and there was a note."

"What'd it say?"

"I don't love you anymore. I can't do this anymore. I'm leaving."

"That's it?"

"Yeah. That's it. Just like that, she's out of our lives."

"Was she seeing someone?" Annie internally kicked herself for hoping, just a little, that she was. Hey, she wasn't perfect. She liked the idea of Dave getting some karma to kick him in the ass.

"Probably. The neighbor saw her peel out of our driveway yesterday morning with a guy who was twentysomething."

"Where was Esmerelda?"

"At day care."

"Day care? Really?"

"Yeah. Melissa said she needed a break from her a few days a week."

"Have things been bad?"

"I don't know. I just thought she was distant because of the baby. It's exhausting, you know. I'm not used to this. I don't even know what the hell I'm doing." Dave was sobbing now. Annie hadn't seen Dave cry. Ever. It was unnerving.

"Listen, Annie, I know I have no right being here. I have no right to ask you for help or to even show up. It's just… I don't know what I'm doing. I don't know how often to change a diaper or feed her or anything. And now her mom's gone, just abandoned her. And I don't know what to do. And I had no one to turn to."

In a way, she hated him for showing up, crawling

back to her to use her for help. It served him right for cheating on her with a woman who then cheated on him.

But the baby. The baby didn't deserve this. What kind of a woman abandoned her own child?

Dave wasn't kidding when he said he didn't know what to do. When Amelia was a baby, Dave was a very hands-off kind of dad. No diapers. Feeding only if Annie warmed the bottle and got it ready. Nothing but the bare minimum participation.

And now he was on his own.

"What do you need?" she heard herself asking, still hating him for what he'd done to her, still hating that he was coming to her after everything.

"I don't know."

Annie sighed, looking at the ceiling in exasperation. She grabbed for the remote with one hand, the baby drifting to sleep in her arms. She clicked off the soap opera, not needing any fictional drama in her life after all. There was clearly real drama all around her. There was a real-life soap opera happening in her living room.

The man who had left her, had cheated on her, had stomped her life into crumbles over a year ago was back. He was back with another woman's baby, with a pleading look in his eye, and a desperation for help Annie could give.

He was back, but she was gone in many ways. She'd left a year ago, her heart given to a new man.

So here they sat, a man, a woman, and a baby in a house that had once belonged to the same man and woman. A house where they had raised their own baby over three decades ago. A house where they had been in love, had made love, and had fallen out of love.

A house that now belonged to her and another man, a man she'd married and was crazy about.

Despite the absurdities of her life, the anger she felt toward Dave, and the oddness of him crying on her couch, she turned to him and said the only thing she could think of.

"Let's start with diapers."

Chapter Seven

Charlotte

"No, don't. I'll take him," Charlotte said as tears streamed down her face.

All around her, the howls of dejected dogs rang out. Cats cried and hissed, and doors clinked as volunteers cleaned the cages. But all Charlotte could hear were the words Glinda had uttered a few minutes ago.

"Horace has to go. His time's up."

When Charlotte had decided to volunteer a few days a week at Second Chances Humane Society, Annie, Amelia, and Leonard had resoundingly told her it was a bad idea.

"Charlotte, it's going to be too hard on you. You know

they can't save every animal there," Leonard had argued.

"He's right, Mom. You know not every cat gets a home. How are you going to feel knowing that?" Annie had added.

"But I have to do something. And if I can't have cats in my house anymore, I can at least help out, try to get them homes. I'm perfect for this job," Charlotte protested over dinner last year when the subject came up. She had seen an ad in the newspaper about how desperately volunteers were needed. It felt like the right thing to do. She certainly had the time.

Charlotte had turned to Amelia, who was also at dinner the day of the discussion.

But Amelia hadn't been on her side, either.

"Grandma, I think it sounds like a great idea and I know you just want to help. But it's going to break your heart when they don't all get adopted. I think it'll be too hard on you, and we don't need anything upsetting you."

Instead of listening to her loved ones, though, Charlotte had dismissed their points... although they were valid, if she were honest.

"This isn't up for discussion. I love animals, and they need help. You're right. I can't help every animal. But I can help some. So I'm doing this."

And so began her bi-weekly volunteer trips to the Humane Society.

Her family had been right. It was tough watching all the cats and dogs abandoned, abused, and rejected by society. When Charlotte brushed a cat or took a dog for a walk, all she saw was innocence and love. How could anyone want to hurt these creatures or throw them away like disposable entities?

There had been beautiful moments along the way. Last-minute rescues, matches made in heaven. There was the feeling that every time she visited and paid attention to the cats there, she was making their day a little bit better.

But then came this morning.

Horace was a large black male cat who had been a stray. He'd been at the shelter since Charlotte had first started volunteering.

She'd seen something in his emerald green eyes on that first day, felt a connection with him when he meowed at her. Although she tried to treat all the cats equally, there was always extra time spent with Horace, extra love, extra scratches.

She'd wanted to bring him home that first week but was met with reluctance from Leonard.

"You know we can't have pets here," he had pragmatically argued.

She had sighed. "I know, but I love him."

"I know you do. But why don't you focus on finding him a good home with someone else?"

And she had.

For months, she'd been trying to promote him to any visitors, to strangers on the street, to her cashier at the grocery store.

But she had failed him.

And now his time was up.

"Glinda, you can't take him. He's only four. It's not his time. Please give him more time."

Glinda, too, had been tearing up. "Char, I know. This is awful. But we don't have the space, and we just don't have any more time for him. We have to follow the policy."

Tears fell from her eyes as she looked into the cage at Horace. His gaze was piercing hers. He let out a quiet, dejected meow as he pawed at her.

And that's when the words came out of her mouth.

"I'll take him."

Glinda stared at her, shaking her head. "Char, you can't. You can't take him."

Charlotte's gaze hardened, her stubborn streak kicking in. "I said I'll take him. Don't worry about how or why. Just know he's not dying today. It's not happening." Charlotte unlocked Horace's cage, reaching in to stroke the cat. She picked him up, propping him over her shoulder. He purred loudly.

"There, there, baby. You're coming home now."

"Charlotte," Glinda argued, but Charlotte ignored her.

"You have my information. Fill out the paperwork. Or don't. But you're not getting him, Glinda. Horace is coming home with me."

A few other workers had gathered at this point to stare at her, but she was done. She knew now why she'd been placed in this volunteer position.

She was meant to rescue Horace. It'd all led up to this.

She didn't look back at their stunned faces. She didn't wait to hear their protests or their discussions of policy. With the heavy black cat in her arms, she marched to the door of Second Chances. And she marched right out, standing in the parking lot to await her ride from Amelia.

***

"Grandma, what are you doing?" Amelia asked when she pulled up to the building and Charlotte got in. She still held on to Horace.

"I'm taking Horace home."

Amelia put the car in park, staring at her.

"What do you mean?"

Charlotte turned to her, still stroking the cat.

"I mean, I'm taking him home."

Amelia sighed. "Grandma, I can't let you take him. You're not allowed to have cats at Wildflower. You know that." The girl reached out to pet the cat, but Charlotte jerked away.

"Listen. They were going to kill him today. End of the road. That's not happening. I failed him by not finding him a home, so I have to make it right. I'm taking him home with me until I figure it out."

"If Cassie sees him, you'll get evicted."

"Then I need your help to make sure she doesn't see him."

"Really? He's huge!"

"Then we just need an extra-large tote bag."

"Are you serious about this?"

"Yes."

Amelia grabbed her head, shaking it. "Okay. This is crazy. I'll help you sneak him in. But Grandma, you can't keep him forever. What're you going to do?"

"Ask Annie to keep him."

"Grandma, no. You can't do that. She already has five. And you know I'd take him, but I can't right now under the circumstances."

"Then I guess I'll just have to keep him under the radar until I can fight the no-pets policy. Besides, the policy can't be that stringent anyway."

"What do you mean?"

"I mean, that witch Catherine has a squawking parakeet in her apartment and no one's said anything about that."

"Grandma, it's a tiny parakeet. It's not hurting anyone."

"And Horace isn't going to hurt anyone either. A pet is a pet. If she gets a parakeet, which wakes me up with its ridiculous chirping at 5:30 a.m., then I should be able to have Horace."

"Grandma, how can the parakeet wake you up? It's way down the hall. And they aren't that loud."

"I have sensitive ears."

"Oh my. Well, let's get rolling. We need to swing by my place and get that tote bag."

Charlotte smiled. "You're the best, dear."

"Don't say that yet. Not until Mission Horace is complete. Now let's go. Looks like today's your lucky day, buddy. You've got the best woman in the world in your corner."

The cat, seeming to understand, meowed.

***

Charlotte tried to walk as casually as possible, Amelia on her right side, Horace weighing down her shoulder. *Please don't meow,* she thought as she tiptoed past Cassie's office.

"Hi, Cassie! Nice day today, huh?" Amelia offered, trying to not call attention to the large, hairy tote bag.

"Yes, gorgeous. Charlotte, can you come here for a second? I have a quick question." Charlotte's heart sank.

"Um, yeah, just let me put these groceries in my apartment, and then I'll be back," she replied.

"Groceries? In that bag? Interesting." Charlotte silently kicked herself. Why the heck would she have groceries in a Grateful Dead tote bag?

"Reduce, reuse, recycle, right?" she offered, shrugging. This appeased Cassie because she just nodded.

Sweat beading on her forehead and arm straining, Charlotte fought the urge to dash to her apartment door. Instead, she walked slowly and confidently to the apartment, unlocked it, and set the bag down inside. Amelia shut the apartment door behind her.

"We did it," Charlotte said, turning to Amelia and smiling. Charlotte leaned against the wall, her arm exhausted from the small trek. Horace was certainly no lightweight.

Footsteps echoed down the hall as Leonard came toward the front of the apartment.

"Hey, honey, how was...." Leonard stopped midsentence when the large black cat approached him, rubbing his leg. "What the?"

"Leonard, meet Horace."

"Charlotte, what are you doing?"

"Now listen, I can explain. Horace was out of time today. And I couldn't bear it. Leonard, he's only four. Can you imagine?"

Leonard just stared at her. "Charlotte."

"Now I know what you're going to say. That we can't possibly keep him. That it's against the rules. But I mean, can't we bend the rules just this once? For a truly worthy cause? Look at him, Leonard. He loves you. And they were going to kill him. Kill him!" She made a killing motion against her neck with her finger.

"Charlotte. We can't keep him."

"It's temporary."

"Until when?"

"Until I find him a home."

"Charlotte. I know you."

"Then you know this is important."

"I know. But we can't do this."

Amelia cleared her throat as the conversation escalated. "Guys, I hate to interrupt, but I really need to get going. I'll give you two time to work this out."

"Thanks, dear," Charlotte replied, stopping to hug her.

"Anytime. Oh, and Grandma?"

"Yes, dear."

"You might want to go get some supplies. Horace

looks like he's searching for a litter box."

They all turned to see Horace meowing in the corner, scratching the carpet as if it were loose litter.

"Oh dear. You're right. I'll have to get some supplies to make him comfortable."

"He's not staying," Leonard retorted.

Charlotte eyed him cautiously. "Well, honey, thanks again. I'll see you out."

She walked Amelia to the door, waving her away into the hallway.

"I'll call you later," she offered, leaving the door open a crack to yell after Amelia. Amelia turned to respond halfway down the hall, but then she started dashing.

"Grandma!" she hissed. Charlotte was confused. And then she remembered. She wasn't used to having to be careful about the door.

She looked down, the door still cracked, to realize why Amelia was panicking.

Horace was running between her legs. She didn't think a cat of that girth could get moving so fast. But now he was sprinting down the hallway.

He passed by Amelia, who tried desperately to catch him to no avail.

The cat kept running, dashing away, Charlotte chasing after him.

He stopped way down the hallway, past the elevator.

He stopped right at the feet of the last person on earth Charlotte wanted to see right then.

"Charlotte Noel, is this your mangy, smelly cat?"

the uppity voice screeched. "Unbelievable! If I get fleas from this beast, you're getting sued."

It was at that exact moment that Horace decided he did, in fact, need to use the litter box.

And Catherine's Jimmy Choo shoe apparently smelled like the perfect litter-like material to him.

**

"Go back to your apartments, everyone. It's all going to be okay," Cassie promised, a fake smile plastered on her face.

After the shriek from Catherine's bright red lips alarmed the entire building, after Leonard had finally captured the cat and rushed him back to their apartment, Cassie's clicking heels had clacked down the hallway toward Charlotte.

"Charlotte, I need to see you in my office. Now."

There wasn't a smile for Charlotte, real or fake.

Now, she sat in Cassie's familiar office with a familiar sight... Catherine by her side.

"Charlotte, you know our policy here. No pets."

Charlotte, although embarrassed about the entire scene in the hallway, was enraged.

"So what exactly is the policy, Cassie? Can you remind me?"

"The policy is no pets running around, idiot. Are you getting Alzheimer's now?" Catherine spat at her, her Jimmy Choos now in the garbage bin in the hallway.

"Well then, Catherine, why do you have a pet?"

"It's a bird. A parakeet. It's in a cage. Quite the

difference from your hell cat that defecated on my $750 shoes. Which you'll be paying me for, I assume."

"I would have defecated on them too if I were Horace."

"Horace? He has a name? Like you're actually going to get to keep him?"

"Keep it up, and I'll send Horace over to shut up your screeching parakeet tomorrow at 5:30 a.m. Am I the only one who hears it? Certainly someone else has complained." Charlotte turned to Cassie on the last statement. Cassie, however, had buried her head in her hands.

"Ladies, please. It's Friday. I'm not ready for this." Bags under Cassie's eyes underscored her exhaustion. The past year had certainly changed her. Although she was still annoyingly happy most of the time and she still found an exorbitant amount of enthusiasm on game nights, the girl looked tired. Charlotte felt a little bit bad about this. It was partially her fault.

"The policy is no pets. That means no cats. No parakeets. No fish. No bugs. Nothing. Now I'm sorry, but Horace and… Tweetie… have to go."

"Tweetie? I would never be that unoriginal. Marilyn."

"Oh my God," she replied. "Really? As in Marilyn Monroe?"

"Of course. And I don't want to hear it. It's better than Horace." Catherine over-enunciated the final syllable.

"Okay, listen, ladies. I'm done here. I'm done." Tears welled in Cassie's eyes.

Charlotte's heart softened. "We're sorry, sweetie. Are

you okay?"

"I will be when you two get rid of your contraband and stop fighting for two seconds. I thought things were better? Aren't you two family now?"

"God no," Catherine blurted.

"Hell no," Charlotte said at the same time.

Cassie raised her eyebrows and gave them a quizzical look. "Okay, I'm not getting into this with you. All I can say is, the pets have to go. You've both got twenty-four hours. I don't want to hear any nonsense about you two still having them. Now I'm trusting you to take care of this."

Charlotte's heart sank as she plodded out of the office. What was she going to do now? She'd have to ask Annie, beg her to take him.

She started heading to her apartment, shoulders slumped, when she heard a "psst." She turned to see Catherine, arms crossed, standing in the hallway.

"Okay, look. I don't want to get rid of Marilyn. And you don't want to get rid of that hell cat."

"Horace."

"Whatever."

"So listen. Let's make a deal. I won't say anything about your chubby, greasy cat if you pretend you don't hear Marilyn in the mornings."

"And why would I trust you?"

"Well, what choice do we have?"

She sighed in resignation. "I guess you're right. But Cassie's going to check for them tomorrow, I'm sure."

Catherine stroked her chin in thought. "Yes, you're right. She's going to check our apartments tomorrow."

The light bulb came on. "Yeah, she'll be checking our apartments, but not anyone else's. So if we could find somewhere to stow them until tomorrow…"

"We could then sneak them back in the next night, and no one would be the wiser."

They looked at each other, smiled, and headed down the hall to knock on Bridget's door.

***

Under the cover of night, Marilyn and Horace were snuck into Bridget's apartment. "Oh, this is so fun! It's like we're Bonnie and Clyde!" she proclaimed when she got the secret signal knock.

"Except you're hiding pets, not cash," Catherine retorted.

"Thanks for doing this," Charlotte said, hugging her friend.

"No problem! They're both adorable."

And with that, Charlotte and Catherine crept back down the dark hallway to their respective homes.

"See, maybe we can get along. Right? Family," Charlotte said, rolling her eyes.

Catherine just kept walking. Before Charlotte opened her door and went back in, she whispered to Charlotte, "Hey, family?"

"Yeah?"

"You still owe me $750."

"Screw you," Charlotte shrieked. She went in,

slamming the door harder than she intended.

"It's done," she said to Leonard, who was watching *Family Feud* in his chair.

"It's hardly done," he said, looking at her.

"Leonard, it's going to be fine. Besides, Horace needed me."

He got up from his chair slowly, leaning on his cane, and traipsed across the living room and kitchen to her.

"Charlotte, I know your heart is in the right place," he started.

"I feel a *but* coming on."

"But Charlotte, you can't save everyone."

Charlotte grimaced. "I know. I know."

"Do you?"

"Yes."

They embraced, but she sensed a tension in the hug, a tension unfamiliar in their relationship.

Chapter Eight

Charlotte

Déjà vu.

That's all Charlotte could think the next morning when she heard Annie utter the same words Catherine had uttered the night before.

"It's none of your business."

Why was everyone so adamant about being private these days?

"Annie, I'm not trying to pry. I'm just worried about you."

"Mom, it's nothing. Nothing's going on. And why the heck is Bridget's daughter's hairdresser spying on me?"

"She's not spying, dear. She lives down the street

from you. And she just so happened to be walking her dog when she saw Dave and… what was her name?"

"Esmerelda."

"Oh my God. Seriously? What was that awful woman thinking?"

"I know."

"But anyway, she saw them. And I'm just wondering what happened, that's all."

"And I said nothing, Mom. It's none of your business."

"Of course it's my business. You're my daughter." Charlotte scratched Horace's neck. He'd survived a night of hiding and a morning inspection. He was back, against Leonard's wishes. Although he had gone out to get some secret Horace supplies. Horace was clearly growing on him.

"Mom, I know. But you've got to stop worrying about me."

"I'm not worried. I just want to make sure you know what you're doing." Horace let out a meow as Charlotte scratched the base of his tail.

"Mom, what was that?"

"Just the television, dear."

Horace, as if on cue, meowed a second time.

"Mom? Do you have a cat?"

"Of course not."

"You know that would be against Wildflower's policy."

"Obviously, dear. That's why it isn't. It's on TV."

"Well, anyway, Mom. I have to go. Someone's at the

door."

"Is it Dave and Esperenza?"

"Esmerelda, Mom."

"Whatever the hideous name is. It's all the same. Is it him?"

"Good-bye, Mom."

"Annie, be careful. I love you."

"I love you too. And please try not to get evicted with your secret cats."

"Will do." The phone clicked. Charlotte hung up.

Secrets. That's all the family seemed to be full of these days, she thought, as she stroked Horace and drifted off to sleep.

***

"I'll have the pasta primavera, please." Charlotte snapped shut her glossy menu, handing the slippery pages to the waitress.

Chewing a large wad of gum, the teenager finished scrawling down Charlotte's order, grabbed the menus, and headed off to the kitchen to turn in Leonard and Charlotte's order.

Charlotte aimlessly took a sip from her water, her mind wandering. What was Annie thinking? Things were finally sorting themselves out. Joe, although he had a mother who was clearly related to the devil, was a nice man. Why would Annie even give that scumbag Dave the time of day, let alone help him out? Yes, it was unfortunate the baby with the ugly name was going to feel the repercussions, but that was Dave's problem.

Charlotte leaped out of her own internal argument at the touch of Leonard's hand on hers.

"Char? Are you listening?"

"Oh, yes, dear, uh-huh."

"Then you agree we need to find Horace a home today?"

"What? Absolutely not!"

Leonard shook his head. "I knew it."

"Knew what?"

"You weren't paying a bit of attention. What are you thinking about in that gorgeous head of yours? Or do I even need to ask?"

Charlotte sighed, fiddling with the paper cover from her straw. "I'm sorry. I know I've been in my own little world lately. It's just, I'm worried. First there was the Amelia situation, and now Annie's going off and making bad decisions. It's just so complicated."

"I know. But Charlotte? You can't make everything okay. You just can't."

She looked up at him now, seeing those eyes that told her everything would be okay. Even if she felt like it wouldn't. She smiled in spite of her inner fears. Leonard did that for her. He was her rock, her foundation in this crazy life. Whatever was happening with Amelia and Annie, whatever they were going through, she was thankful for one thing.

Her life with Leonard was strong.

She leaned across the table now to give him a quick kiss. On her way back to her seat, she almost knocked

LINDSAY DETWILER

over her water, but Leonard's quick thinking caught it.

"I'm sorry, honey. I hate that I've been neglecting us lately."

"It's okay. I know you just love your girls. I get it. But I do miss having you mostly to myself." He winked at her.

"You're right, though. I can't make it all okay. I can just be here for them. Things aren't going to be perfect."

"That's right."

"I'm sorry, Leonard. I'm sorry we had to cancel our trip."

"About that."

She raised an eyebrow. "About what? The trip?"

"I talked to the travel agency. There's been a cancellation for next week's trip. We'd be staying at a different place than we planned, but the tourist attractions are pretty much the same. It's not too late. We could reschedule," he said, pleading with her with his eyes.

She took a deep breath. "Leonard, that sounds wonderful. I really want this trip. But I know if we go now, I won't enjoy it. Can we please wait, just a while, until things settle down?"

Disappointment registered on his face, but his gentle demeanor covered it with a smile. "I had a feeling you'd say that. I understand. I do. We'll go another time."

"Thank you. I love you."

"I love you too."

Their food came, and they dove in, talking about the upcoming quilting party at Wildflower and what color

68

collar they should get for Horace. Things were back on track, Charlotte told herself, Ireland or not. Leonard was patient and understanding. He understood that family had to come first.

But as the conversation rolled on and she stuffed the pasta into her mouth, Charlotte couldn't help but notice the wistful look in Leonard's eyes, the sad, silent despondence certainly a result of their cancellation.

We'll go eventually, she thought, smiling at Leonard who was now cleaning a spot of sauce off of his new shirt.

But there was a nagging in her head saying she didn't know if that was true.

***

When they got back to Wildflower, all the lights were out, only the safety lights illuminating the hallway. It was late, at least by Wildflower standards. Leonard and Charlotte walked hand in hand, trying to avoid the squeaky spots in the hallway they had memorized. Before they got to their door, however, Charlotte put a hand in front of Leonard, stopping him.

"Do you hear that?"

"Hear what?"

"Shh, listen."

They paused, listening intently for the mystery sound.

A muffled noise was coming from the community room. It was an odd noise. Not footsteps, not really voices. Just a slight, muffled banging noise followed by some strange gasping noises.

"What is that?" Leonard asked, looking at Charlotte in the darkness. "Should we call Cassie?"

"There's no time. Someone could be in trouble. Let's go," Charlotte responded, leading the way down the other hallway to the community room.

Leonard and Charlotte crept as silently as possible, just in case they were heading into the grasp of a robber instead of heading to a fallen resident's aid.

What is with this potential robber scare lately? Charlotte thought.

When they got to the entrance to the room, Leonard motioned for Charlotte to stay back, putting a finger to his lips to warn her to be quiet. She nodded, back flat against the wall, hopefully out of sight.

Leonard snuck along the corner, trying to creep into the community room to gauge the scene.

He turned back to Charlotte after a moment and whispered, "I don't see anything."

The noise, however, was still enduring, still unidentifiable.

Charlotte crept behind Leonard as they wandered deeper into the room, the noise getting slightly louder.

"I think it's coming from the coat closet back there," she whispered, pointing Leonard toward the back corner of the room.

He looked at Charlotte, puzzled, but they continued on. They were committed now.

They crept to the closet, Charlotte wondering if this was such a good idea.

"Maybe we should call the police," she whispered, but Leonard just batted the idea away. "It's fine. Let's just figure it out," he said.

Men. Always having to play the hero.

They carefully approached the closet door, the muffled noises definitely louder now.

And then what sounded like a shriek rang in the closet. Charlotte and Leonard jumped.

"That's it," she announced, loud enough for the victim or perpetrator to hear her. Charlotte brushed by Leonard, ignoring his warnings, and flung open the closet door.

Horrified screams erupted from the closet and Charlotte at the same time. Leonard gasped. Another male voice said, "What the hell?" Charlotte and Leonard froze, baffled, embarrassed. There were more expletives from the closet as Charlotte tried to back away, covering her eyes.

"Oh my God!" she exclaimed.

It was too late, though, for Charlotte to meander back to her apartment and unsee what she'd just seen. Because by now, other residents had wandered into the community room.

Someone flipped the light switch just in time for Charlotte, Leonard, and several other residents to see Catherine sprawled on the floor trying to readjust her dress. Behind her lay the newest Wildflower resident, pants around his ankles, also squirming to reclothe himself.

"Do you have to ruin everything?" Catherine blurted

when she finally managed to stand, her face red and angry.

"What the hell were you doing in there? Don't you have a bed of your own?" Charlotte retorted, embarrassed by the situation but determined it wasn't her fault.

By this time, Randall, Catherine's closet pal, had also stood, brushing himself off. He towered over Catherine, his arms bracing her.

He was at least twenty-five years younger than Catherine, and it showed in his stance. He looked like a body builder compared to Leonard. Age was simply on his side.

"It is none of your business what I do and where I do it, thank you."

"It is when I have to see it," Charlotte responded, voice rising.

"Well, mind your own damn business and you won't have to," Catherine huffed. "What're you all looking at? Everything's fine here. I mean, I know everyone probably wants a glance at all of this, but he's mine. Move along." She motioned toward Randall as if she were Vanna White showing off the next word puzzle. Charlotte just chortled.

"All right, our mistake. Sorry," Leonard apologized.

"Don't apologize. They're the nasty ones having sexcapades in the community room. Disgraceful."

"You're just jealous." Catherine winked, pulling Randall behind her. "Come on, Randall. Let's go somewhere we won't make other, washed-up, dried-up residents jealous." She shot Charlotte a wide smile and sashayed out of the community room, leading a grinning Randall behind her.

Charlotte groaned.

"Unbelievable. What? Does she think she's twenty?"

She turned to hear what Leonard would add to the conversation, but he was just looking at her, eyes sparkling.

"You know, maybe it's not such a bad idea," he whispered, leaning in to kiss her.

"Are you serious right now?" She was appalled. How could he be thinking about anything but how disgraceful Catherine was? And the nerve of her to act like they were in the wrong.

But then Leonard started kissing her, and she realized it was nice to let her mind slip away, even if temporarily.

No worrying about Annie and Amelia. No stressing over Catherine's ridiculous escapades.

Just Leonard's lips on hers, warmth buzzing.

"Who needs Ireland?" she asked as he responded with his lips touching hers. "Let's go home." Leonard nodded, shutting the closet door in the community room.

She led him back to their apartment after looking at the closet door with disdain.

"Someone should probably tell Cassie to Lysol that tomorrow," she said as they walked away.

Leonard laughed. "I don't know if I want to be the one to tell Cassie what was happening in her closet."

Charlotte laughed, not worrying that it reverberated

through the hallway. If Wildflower was asleep already, they certainly weren't after Catherine's closet rendezvous.

That was what she loved about this place. They might be old, they might be tired.

But they were never, ever boring.

Chapter Nine

Amelia

"Can you paint skulls?" Amelia asked as the Chinese nail technician tilted his head. "You know, death? Skulls?" She pointed to her head, taking a finger and pretending to pull it across her throat.

The technician looked to his friend as if asking for help.

"Forget it. Flowers will be fine." She smiled, the technician looking more relaxed as he began painting pink flowers on the black background.

Janie giggled. "Not sure skulls is the message you're looking to send right now, is it? I mean, it's not that bad, right?"

Amelia sighed. "No, it's not. I don't want you getting the wrong impression. I *am* in love with your brother. And I *am* excited about this baby. Please don't think I'm a terrible mother."

"I wasn't. Come on, Amelia. Stop being so hard on yourself."

"Well, in all honesty, I am thinking exactly that. I have no clue what I'm doing." Amelia stared blankly at the pink designs taking shape on her nails.

"It'll be fine. Seriously. Owen's crazy about you. Just give him a chance. You can figure this out together."

The two women sat in silence for a few moments as the two men at Nice Nails, Inc., continued to work. Amelia hadn't had a manicure in years, but Janie had insisted they take a break and relax. She insisted they needed this.

Amelia had expected things to be weird with Janie after the accidental revealing of her secret... which happened to involve Janie's brother. There had been a few hours of avoidance the following morning, a few odd glances and tense pauses.

And then Janie had said, "Okay. Let's cut the crap. I'm not going to tiptoe around you. You're having a baby with my brother. That's fantastic. And you might be nervous and worried. But you're being crazy. Owen's nuts about you. I know a baby is a scary thing. But seriously. This is awesome. Welcome to the family." Amelia stood, stunned, as Janie wrapped her arms around her. She gently hugged her back.

And the awkwardness was over.

Amelia loved that about Janie. It was a trait also familiar in Owen. It was like neither Owen nor Janie had time to be someone they weren't, to say something they didn't mean, or to hide something they wanted to say. There were no secrets or hidden agendas. There was just in-your-face, sometimes brutal honesty.

So Amelia shouldn't have been surprised by Janie's next statement. She should have seen it coming. It was foolish of her to think otherwise. But it still slapped her in the face when Janie uttered the words, caused her to feel nauseous. Caused her to knock over the nail polish, which, in turn, caused the nail technician to explode with expletives in both Chinese and English.

Because when Janie turned to Amelia matter-of-factly and said, "Owen knows about the baby," Amelia couldn't help but feel like the flowers on her nails had, in fact, morphed into skulls with crossbones. She saw the flowery meadow of "it'll all be all right" transform into a dead field. She saw her relationship with Owen dry up, shriveled and wilted, before her eyes.

***

Janie gave the two technicians an extra-large tip as Amelia sulked near the door, thoughts and worries swirling in her mind. When Janie headed out the door, the bells tinkling, Amelia followed like an insolent teenager.

In the car, Amelia buckled her seat belt, sinking down in her seat. After a moment, she turned to Janie and spewed, "How could you? This wasn't your secret."

"He had to know."

"First you eavesdrop. And now this? How dare you mess with my life."

"I'm helping it." Janie put on her sunglasses as she shrugged. She was unapologetic and stoic in her responses.

"Helping it by revealing my secret? This is my business, not yours."

"He's my brother. Look, Amelia, I think you're awesome and I think you're going to be a fantastic sister-in-law. But he's my *brother*. My loyalty is with him, and he deserved to know. You'll thank me."

"Thank you? Are you fucking kidding? And who says we're getting married? Stay out of our lives."

Janie turned up the music to Amelia's anger. She looked left and right before pulling out into the parking lot.

"I can't do that."

"Excuse me?"

"I can't stay out of your life. Because I care about you both too much to let you screw this up."

"Well what am I supposed to do now?"

"Talk to him."

"I'm not ready for that."

"You have to be."

"Well I'm not."

"Too bad. Because he's on his way home."

Amelia froze, panic erupting deep inside. "What?"

"Yeah. His flight's in a few hours."

"Great. Just great."

"Amelia, stop being ridiculous. You love each other. What's the problem? It could be a whole lot worse, you know."

"And how the hell would you know anything about this?"

Janie pulled to the stop sign, not worrying about any traffic behind her. She put the car in park, pulled her sunglasses from her eyes, and gaped at Amelia.

"I know a whole lot about carrying the child of a man who is an abusive prick. I know all about being afraid your boyfriend is going to beat you and your baby to death. And I know what it's like to miscarry that baby and have a boyfriend simply say 'good.' So yeah, it could be a lot worse. This might not be the fairy tale you dreamed about. But it could be so much worse."

Amelia's stomach plummeted, and she had no clue what to say. She felt like a total bitch now. Janie was right. What was she freaking out about? Owen loved her. Things would be fine. She had nothing to complain about.

"I'm sorry," Amelia murmured, tearing up in spite of herself.

Janie shoved the glasses back on her face with one finger. She mustered up a smile. "Don't be. I'm not trying to make you feel bad. I'm just trying to put it in perspective. Things aren't that bad. It's going to be fine. Now, enough tears. How about some milkshakes before we get home?"

Amelia found herself nodding, both at the prospect of milkshakes and at the prospect that Janie was perhaps the best thing to come into her life, next to Owen of course.

No matter what, it will be all right, she thought, as they pulled into Tasty Freezes for the two biggest chocolate shakes they could order.

Chapter Ten

Amelia

"Amelia?"

Amelia groggily opened her eyes, her hands instinctually rubbing her face as the sun poured through the cheap blinds. She felt a firm hand on her shoulder, shaking her. She smelled a familiar cologne, recognized his touch.

Her eyes opened and her gaze landed on him.

Owen.

He was here in their bed. He was home.

She sat up, tousling her hair as he leaned in, embracing her completely. They held each other for a while. It felt good to have his warmth around her, to rest her face in his neck. It felt good to have his hands rustling her hair, know the safety of his strength. It didn't matter that her hair was all over the place or that she hadn't brushed her teeth. All that mattered was the electricity between them, an electricity she had almost forgotten in the past few days.

He pulled back gently, his gaze piercing hers. She smiled in spite of herself.

"Why didn't you tell me?" His words shifted the tone. She stared straight ahead, the smile slowly dissipating

"I didn't know what to say."

"Amelia, we're having a baby. Me and you. You didn't have to say anything special. You just had to say it." His smile was warm and genuine. Her heart loosened a bit, her chest breathing a sigh of relief. She had imagined a cold, harsh reaction, a disappointment flooding his eyes.

But all she saw was joy.

Tears filled her eyes, partially from the emotional quality of the conversation, partially from the relief. "I didn't think you wanted this. After our conversation last week, I—"

He cut her off, hushing her with a touch. "That was different. That was when it wasn't real. But it *is* real. We're having a baby. How could I not want this? I love you. Yeah, this isn't what we'd imagined, not yet. But I'm crazy about you. There's no one else I'd rather take this journey with."

The kiss that followed was a kiss to wipe her worries away, a kiss to make her forget she'd ever doubted their love, their life, their relationship. With one kiss, Owen reminded her of why she fell in love with him, why it would all be okay.

The kiss intensified. As good as it felt to have Owen leaning over the top of her, as tempting as it was, she put a hand on his chest to stop him.

"Owen, wait. Your sister… we can't…."

He smiled, still devouring her lips, only stopping to say, "She went shopping."

Amelia smiled into his lips, passion pulling her into him.

For the next hour, Owen and Amelia lay in their bed, coming full circle to the place they had begun. There wasn't talk of cribs and day care, of what now and what next. There was just Owen, the crazy Adam Levine lookalike, and Amelia, the black-wearing songwriting girl.

That was all they needed right then.

***

"Smells amazing," Amelia muttered into his neck as he flipped the bacon a few hours later. The sizzling of the bacon coupled with the glorious scent made Amelia's stomach leap. She was starving. He grinned as she kissed his neck.

"Any weird cravings yet?" He turned from the pan to look at her.

"I'm not that far along yet."

"Have you been to the doctor yet?"

"I'm making an appointment today."

"'Kay, just let me know when."

"It's just an appointment."

"And I'm going to be there." He took a step away from the stove, turning to wrap her in his arms. "I'm serious. I'm going to be there for everything. I love you."

"I love you too."

Owen continued playing house husband, finishing breakfast, refusing to let her help. She propped herself on the couch in front of the morning news, smiling as her hand instinctually fell to her stomach. With the scent of bacon filling the kitchen, she tucked her legs underneath her on the couch. Things were good. She had a man in the kitchen willing to move heaven and earth for her and their child, a man who adored her. A man who would adore their baby.

Sitting there thinking about it, she realized how silly she was for worrying at all. She'd been crazy to think Owen would be anything but a perfect partner, a perfect dad.

She should've known he'd drop everything to be here for her, for them.

But then again, wasn't that what she was afraid of all along?

She didn't have time to wonder because before she could drift too far into her own thoughts, the door swung open.

"Owen!" Janie proclaimed, dropping her shopping bags to run over to her big brother.

"Hey," he said as he put the plates of bacon and eggs

on the counter.

They embraced as Amelia stood up from the couch, sauntering over to breakfast with her family.

***

Shoving bacon in her mouth, Janie continued talking about residencies and night shifts and hospital departments as Owen and Amelia listened. The girl was always animated, but she was even more animated now that her big brother was here, Amelia noticed. Amelia smiled at the warmth of their sibling bond.

"So enough about me. Tell me about your tour, big brother. Where are you guys off to next? So awesome that this is happening for you."

Amelia slurped on her orange juice, eying Owen. She detected a hint of reluctance on his face, but she was probably imagining it. He averted his eyes to his eggs, aimlessly pushing them around with his fork.

Amelia spoke up for him. "Oh, I think it's Brazil next, isn't it? When is the concert there again? I forget."

Owen looked up at her, a slight grin on his face. "I don't know."

"Well you better figure it out, *sí*?" Janie teased as she continued shoveling food in.

"I don't know because I'm not going. The guys will have to figure it out."

Amelia and Janie both paused, giving each other sideways glances.

Amelia spoke first. "What do you mean you're not going? Owen, that's crazy. You're the lead singer. You can't just skip it."

He put his fork down, looking at her, a smile plastered on his face. "Not anymore."

She tilted her head in disbelief. "What?"

"I quit the band." He shrugged, reaching for his fork, but Amelia slapped his hand down, making him look at her.

"What do you mean, you quit?" Trepidation crept into her voice.

"I'm done. I told the guys yesterday they need to find someone new. I have other priorities now." Owen smiled at her, the revelation coming off his tongue as calmly and simply as if he were telling her the weather forecast. Janie just looked at him, admiration evident in her eyes.

"I think that's great, big brother."

Amelia glared at her. "What the hell are you talking about? Are you two crazy? Your band is finally taking off, and you quit? What the hell?"

"It doesn't matter anymore. All that matters are you and the baby. I can't be on the road touring all the time while you're back here. And the tour life is no life for raising a child. So I made a decision. I want this. There was never a question. As soon as I heard, I knew I was done. No looking back."

Tears started welling in Amelia's eyes. She pushed herself back from the table, heading to the counter. She leaned on it heavily, nausea rising.

"Hey, what's wrong? What is it?" He came up behind her, resting his hand on her shoulder. She pushed it away.

"I knew this would happen. I knew it. This is why I couldn't tell you."

"Amelia, what's wrong? I thought you'd be happy. We're getting the life everyone wants. We're going to be happy."

"No, Owen, we're not. We're getting the life I didn't want for us. The conventional, married, settled down with kids life, at the expense of our dreams. You've quit the best thing that ever happened to you, and it's because of me."

"I'm going to go for a walk, give you two some privacy," Janie muttered, reaching for her coat. Owen and Amelia were silent until they heard the door shut.

Owen turned Amelia now, wrapping her in his arms. "Amelia, I have what I want right here. Yeah, you're right. We thought we were going to live the tour life for a while, live that dream. But dreams change. And as soon as I heard about this baby, this miracle, things changed for me. It didn't matter anymore. All that matters are you and this baby, the life we're going to have together."

Tears rolled down Amelia's cheeks as she stared into his face.

"It matters to me. It definitely matters to me."

He stepped back, confusion flooding his face. She brushed by him, her sobs filling the apartment as she rushed back to their bedroom.

He must have sensed her need for space because he left her alone for a while. In their bed, thoughts swirled around her, mostly of how much he would resent her down the road for this decision. But in truth, thoughts of how much she resented the decision swirled as well.

She'd walked away from a man who wanted a conventional life to be with one who didn't. Now, though, she found out Owen and Neville weren't that different at all.

Chapter Eleven

Annie

"Hot chocolate for your thoughts?" Joe asked as Annie glanced up, smiling. She reached her mitten-covered hand toward the steamy liquid, thankful for the warmth.

"My feet are killing me," she admitted, clinking an ice skate against the ground as Joe slinked onto the bench beside her.

"We're getting too old for this."

"You might be, but I'm not," she teased, nudging him with her elbow. He put his arm around her, pulling her close.

"This is nice. I've missed this."

She pulled back to look at him quizzically. "Missed

what?"

"Us. This. Just us, out together, focusing on each other."

She smiled, leaning in to brush her nose on his. "It's been crazy lately, huh?"

"Yeah. Between work and Amelia, it has been."

They sat together for a while, Annie leaning her head on Joe's shoulder, wrapped in the warmth of his body. She'd missed this too, the simplicity of life with Joe. Walks in the park, dates at the indoor skating rink, dinner and movies.

Not that they hadn't been out on dates lately. It was just, if she were being honest, she'd been feeling a bit distracted lately. And she felt a little guilty too.

Because what Joe didn't know, what he couldn't know, was why Annie was so distracted, so tired.

Yes, work was certainly busy with six Christmastime weddings on the calendar. But what was really keeping her busy, keeping her exhausted, was the visitor she had a few times a week.

In actuality, the two visitors she had, two visitors who desperately needed her.

She'd tried to tell Dave "no," tried to tell him he'd have to figure it out himself, but then Esmerelda gave her those eyes. She realized she *needed* to help, not for Dave, but for the baby. The baby needed her. Who else was going to help?

She'd tried to tell Joe about it when it first began, tried to turn to him. She hated keeping secrets.

But she just couldn't.

Something about the situation felt suspicious, even to her. She had no ill intentions, no desire to get back with her ex. But she felt like no matter how she told him, Joe would never be okay with this. He would never believe this was an innocent childcare arrangement, a friend helping a friend.

Maybe if she were being truthful, she didn't quite believe it either.

Because even though it was her ex, even though it wasn't her baby, and even though she loved Joe, there was too much history between Annie and Dave for it to be completely innocent.

***

"Scone, dear?" Charlotte offered the next morning when Annie stopped by to check on her and Leonard.

Since Charlotte's marriage, Annie didn't worry about Charlotte as much. She had eased out of the schedule and habit of checking on Charlotte so frequently, soothed by the fact Leonard was always with her. In fact, sometimes Annie felt silly stopping by at all. She felt like she was intruding. But she still liked visiting her mom. Truth be told, she needed her mom now more than ever.

She'd wanted to confide in Amelia but knew the girl was too closely tied to the situation. Amelia didn't need any extra stress, what with the whole Owen-quitting-the-band scenario. The girl was going through enough of a rough patch. She didn't need to get fired up about Dave. Plus, she still held so much resentment for her father, still basically refused to have him in her life. This would just complicate her anger even more.

"No thanks, Mom. I'm actually here for some advice," she said, pushing away the scone and clinging to her cup of coffee.

Leonard had gone downstairs to play shuffleboard with George and Paul. Annie had her mom all to herself, which was exactly what she needed.

"Well, it must be bad if you're looking to me for advice," Charlotte said. Horace meowed from down the hallway.

Annie was temporarily distracted. "How haven't you got caught yet? That cat has the biggest mouth."

"Well, dear, a perk of living here I suppose. Half the residents are half deaf." Horace trotted over to Charlotte, knowing his piece of scone was coming. Charlotte didn't disappoint. "Now, spill. What's wrong?"

Annie took a sip of her coffee before beginning. "It's Dave. Well, and Joe. It's… well, it's a mess."

Charlotte half coughed at the mention of Dave's name. "Do not tell me, Annie, that you're still seeing Dave. What's going on?"

"It isn't like you think."

"And what am I thinking? That you're sneaking behind your new husband's back to be with that snake of an ex of yours?"

"Mom, I'm not with him. I'm helping him."

"After he screwed you over? Are you out of your mind?"

"Mom, he needs me. More than that, the baby needs me. He has no clue what he's doing. He needs help."

Charlotte gave her a condescending look. "Really? Are you really that naïve?"

"Mom, there's nothing between us."

"Nothing?"

"No, why would there be? I love Joe. End of story."

"Have you told Joe about this little setup?"

Annie just shook her head.

"And why not?"

"I just don't think he'd understand."

"Of course he wouldn't, darling. I'd worry if he did."

"So you think I should tell him?"

"Absolutely not."

Annie looked at Charlotte, confused. "What?"

"Absolutely not. He'll never understand. I surely wouldn't."

"Then what should I do?"

"Tell Dave to stop coming over. Tell him you never want to see him again."

"It's not that simple, Mom."

"It should be. If you love Joe."

"Of course I love Joe." Annie's voice reflected a hint of anger.

"Then it should be easy to tell your ex to go away. Because, Annie, you're just flirting with danger here. You're going to screw this up with Joe, and I would hate to see that happen. You've finally gotten back to being your old self, better than your old self, with him this past year. Don't risk messing it up for a man who doesn't deserve the time of day from you."

Annie rested her head in her hand. "You're right."

"Of course I am, dear."

Annie gave her a glare. "Thanks. I think."

"You're welcome. Now, how about we head downstairs. There's a new dance instructor, and his class starts in twenty minutes."

"His? A male instructor?"

"Yes," Charlotte said, a mischievous grin on her face.

"I don't think I want to go."

"Of course you do. I've heard he looks just like Usher." Charlotte winked.

"And what happened to your crush on Adam Levine?"

"Well, since my granddaughter is having a baby with his doppelganger, I thought maybe I should get a new fantasy crush."

"So you have a crush on Usher? Weren't you just lecturing me about being faithful?"

"See, that's where you've got it all wrong. I *may* have a crush on an Usher lookalike after dance class."

"But it's still a crush. And you're married."

"Right, dear. But the thing is, Leonard knows there's no chance for Usher-lookalike and me. He's in his twenties."

"Isn't Catherine dating a much younger man?"

Charlotte rolled her eyes. "Don't bring up that stupid woman. I was having a fine day. Don't ruin it."

"Okay, but anyway, you shouldn't go to class just to

eye up the man candy."

"That's what I was getting to, dear. I may have a crush on the man candy, but there's no way anything will ever happen. There's nothing between us. So it doesn't hurt to look."

"Well, there's nothing left between Dave and me," Annie argued.

Charlotte turned and looked at her. "That's where you're wrong. That's where you've got it all wrong. You had decades together. Of course there's still something there. And with you, there's definitely a chance for something. That's what makes this so wrong."

Charlotte headed back down the hallway, practicing her Latin hips as Annie stood in the middle of the kitchen, hands in her pockets.

She hated it when her mother was right. She hated it so much.

***

Annie and Joe sat on the park bench down the street from their home, sipping coffee. Annie leaned into him, basking in the warmth of his body and the comfort of having him close. He leaned over to kiss her cheek as they watched a mother frantically chasing after her kids. She hated to destroy this peaceful moment, but her mother was right. Her conversation with Charlotte had sunk in over the past day. She needed to be honest with Joe.

"Can I talk to you about something?" Annie asked, breaking the moment. She had nothing to hide, nothing to be ashamed of, yet the fluttering in her chest told her otherwise.

"Actually, I wanted to talk to you about something too." His eyes sparkled as he turned to her.

"You go first," she offered, curiosity getting the best of her now.

"You sure?"

"Positive. What's up?"

Joe took her hand in his, stroking it with his thumb. "I've been thinking a lot lately about us, about our life. It's crazy how much our lives have changed. Not long ago, we both had given up on love. And now look at us, look at what we've found."

Annie smiled, but her stomach dropped, guilt surging.

"It's just… I've been thinking a lot about what I've missed all these years. And…." Joe fidgeted with what appeared to be nerves. Used to Joe being calm and collected, Annie was troubled.

"What is it? You're scaring me."

"Sorry. I just don't know how you're going to take this."

"Like I said, you're scaring me."

Joe squeezed her hand. "Okay. How would you feel about kids?"

Annie restrained herself from choking. This was not what she'd been thinking he was going to say. It wasn't even on her radar.

"Kids?" It was the only word she could manage.

"I know, it seems kind of crazy. I know Amelia's

getting ready to have a baby, so it seems kind of weird. But it's just… I never had the chance to experience that, to be a dad. Up until last year, I didn't think it was ever going to be a possibility. But then I found you, and we have this amazing life together. You've shown me what I've been missing, shown me what's possible. I've seen the bond you have with Amelia. I think it's something I want."

Annie turned to look at the park nearby. Kids were climbing on monkey bars as exhausted-looking moms and dads chased after them.

She exhaled before turning back to Joe. "It's a lovely sentiment, Joe, and I want to make you happy. But my childbearing days are over."

"Well, I know that. And I know a baby or even toddler might be a bit much at this point in our lives. But what about an older child?"

"What, are you talking about fostering or adopting?"

"Yeah. Why not? I mean, think about what we could do for a teenager. Think about the family we could create together."

Annie's heart was moved by Joe's excitement and warmth. He was just the kind of man to want to do something so generous. His heart was truly big.

She thought the idea was beautiful. She could see them together, helping give a child a family—even if it was sometimes dysfunctional. She could see Joe as an amazing father figure.

But her heart wasn't quite there. There was so much

to think about.

Lately, life was so tiresomely complex. The situation with Dave, Amelia's panic over the baby, everything swirled together into a cacophony of worries in her mind. She was struggling with so much right now. She couldn't imagine adding anything else.

She wanted to tell Joe right then. She wanted to tell him why she felt stressed, why she couldn't quite jump headfirst into this. Glancing at him, though, this trusting man who had put so much of his heart into them, who wanted to grow with her into a family, she felt her words shrivel.

This was not the right moment, she decided, knowing she was avoiding the task because she didn't want to hurt him. She couldn't tell him about Dave now, she just couldn't.

"I love your enthusiasm. I just…. I thought my child raising days were over, you know? This just caught me off guard. Can I take some time and think about it?"

"Of course. I didn't expect us to jump right in. I'm just glad you're willing to think about it." He hugged her then, seemingly content with her answer.

He patted her knee before pulling back, the two of them now facing the playground again. She was sure Joe was facing the playground with a new set of eyes, a new hope.

"So what did you want to tell me?"

She turned to face him, told herself this was it. She needed to tell him the truth about Dave.

But instead, she simply said, "Never mind. Wasn't important."

He raised an eyebrow as if wondering if he should press her further, but apparently decided against it.

"I love you," he whispered into her hair as the children's shrieks ricocheted off the pavement.

"Love you, too," she said, with a wearisome note she hoped he couldn't detect.

Chapter Twelve

Annie

"Macy, are you sure you don't mind?"

"No, it's fine. You've been working so hard on the Janson wedding and everything. Not a big deal. I've got the linen meeting covered. Although I'm sure I'll be regretting it when Mrs. Orion starts freaking out about the thread count in the napkins."

Annie chuckled. "You're the best boss. Thanks again. I'll see you in a few hours."

"I know I'm the best. But you're pretty great too. See you later. Enjoy the morning."

Annie hit End on her cell phone, brushing away a strand of her bangs in frustration. She paused at the kitchen window, looking into the backyard as Butternut sat, also looking out the window at birds.

"What am I doing?" she said to the cat. The cat looked up at her, eyes half closing. Apparently Butternut was wondering the same thing.

She sauntered over to her coffeemaker, no longer in such a hurry to get out the door and get to the linens meeting with her clients. With the morning now off, she should be feeling a bit more relaxed. Joe was at work, and she had the house to herself.

But she wasn't relaxed. She was anything but. And the house wouldn't be all to herself for long.

Annie hadn't called off because she needed to take Butternut to the vet like last Tuesday. She didn't call off to languish in her husband's arms all morning. She didn't call off, like she suggested to Macy, because her migraine was too much to handle.

No, she had called off for a much more sketchy reason.

Five minutes later, the doorbell rang, underscoring the reason for her playing hooky. Her head, though, now truly did feel fogged. She was encroaching on dangerous territory, lying now to Joe and her boss. She was making excuses, making reasons that it was okay for Dave to come over this morning. But deep down, squealing to get out, was the truth Annie couldn't face.

This was a very, very, very bad idea.

***

"Annie, thanks again. I'm so sorry to bother you. I hope we're not interrupting," Dave announced as he handed Esmerelda to Annie on his way in the house.

"No, no, it's fine." It wasn't odd for her to be holding

Esmerelda anymore. She had done this dozens of times now. She realized how natural the baby felt in her arms.

"I really wouldn't have called you if I had any other options. It's just I have this appointment with a client in half an hour and I can't take her with me. The day care doesn't have enough room to take her every day of the week, not this year with such short notice. They're understaffed and at their limit, and they can't make an exception. The girl who usually babysits for me is sick, and I just didn't know what else to do, and…."

"It's fine, Dave. Really." Annie cut him off, a hint of a smile creeping on her face. Dave looked terrible. He was ragged, and he was stressed. He still had no clue what he was doing.

Dave sighed, rustling his fingers through his hair. "I was a fool, you know? Not appreciating you when I had you. How did you manage all this? How does anyone do it? I can't even think straight, let alone manage this. I feel like a piece of shit." His tone hardened as he got to the end of his words, and Annie could see how much this bothered him. Dave was a perfectionist, a go-getter. He never failed at anything. In fact, he was seemingly a natural at everything he tried. From carnival games to foosball to anything else he put his hands on, he got it quickly.

Parenting, well, that was a different story.

He'd never had to go it alone, though. When Amelia was little, Annie had been the caregiver, even after she went back to work. She was the one Amelia came crying to in the middle of the night. She was the one who soothed Amelia when she had a fever or taught her how to tie her shoes. It wasn't that Dave purposefully tried to be a hands-off father or that he didn't love his daughter. It was just different. He was the breadwinner, the one with the career, while Annie had the job. It just made sense that she was the one to deal with the stresses of childrearing so he could be fresh-minded at work.

Now, though, it was coming back to haunt him because now he was forced to go it alone.

But he wasn't alone. No, he had come back to Annie, leaning on her. True, she was angry sometimes when she thought about how she was good enough for him now. She knew she should feel used and angry. But underneath that layer of mistrust and questioning, Annie felt something else.

She felt good.

It was a strange sensation, one she would never admit to anyone else. But it felt good to be needed now by Dave. After being thrown away by him. After the pain of feeling like she wasn't good enough, the betrayal, and being traded in for a younger model, it felt good to be the foundation in his life again. It was satisfying to be the one he was crawling back to.

She hadn't disillusioned herself. She knew this wasn't about them or a relationship or him feeling sorry. It was about Dave needing someone to turn to, someone to help with his daughter. Who else would he pick? She'd been his best friend for three decades. She'd been the one he'd tangled his life with for years. Even though he'd thrown it away, it seemed natural he'd come back to her now.

She still felt guilty for lying to Joe; that while he was working, she was with Dave in the house they used to share.

She reminded herself nothing was happening. This wasn't the rekindling of a love match. This wasn't the fanning of old, familiar flames. It was about the welfare of a child. It was about Annie helping Amelia's half-sister. It was about friendship, forgiveness.

But as Annie waved Dave good-bye, seeing him out the door as she and Esmerelda stood in the doorway, she couldn't help but feel a quiver in her heart. A flashback to another time, another life, grabbed hold of her. Suddenly, it was Amelia in her arms, not Esmerelda. She was younger, firmer, crazy about the man heading to his Corvette. She was the woman Dave came home to and made love with every night; he was the man she couldn't imagine life without. Just for a second, she wasn't the Annie he threw away. Just for a second, her heart fluttered at the prospect.

The engine roared to life as Dave hurried off to his job, and Annie headed in the house to entertain the baby for an hour. As she talked to her and cooed, she caught a glimpse of the picture on the fireplace, a picture that now replaced the one from a lifetime ago.

The picture of Joe smiled at her, and her heart chilled at its core.

No, nothing was physically happening here. But if she

weren't careful, she would be swept away by a nostalgia too strong to fight. She would be whisked out of the life she'd found with Joe, a life she loved, and into the trap that was Dave.

"I won't let it happen," she said to herself as much as to Esmerelda. The baby just looked at her with sparkling green eyes.

***

"I can't thank you enough. You're a lifesaver." Dave reached for Esmerelda when he burst through the door. Annie noted he didn't even knock. But why would he? This was once his house. *Stop overanalyzing,* she scolded herself.

"It's not a problem."

"Let me pay you."

"Get out of here," she teased. She shook her head.

"At least let me buy you lunch?"

"I have to get back to work soon."

"Oh, Annie, did you call off?"

"No. I just asked to go in a little late. It's fine. Macy's flexible."

Dave smiled at her. "So you like your new job?" There was genuine interest in his eyes.

She nodded. "It's what I was always meant to do. I love it. It completes me."

"I love seeing you so passionate about something. I love how you light up when you talk about it. I wish you'd found this job sooner."

Annie paused, afraid to say what was on her mind.

She ignored her inner worries, though, and went all in. "Would it have made a difference?" There was a despondency creeping into her. She felt it wash over her.

"What?"

"If I'd been more passionate, more full of life, would you have stayed?"

He rocked the baby in his arms, looking at her seriously now. "Annie, let's not do this."

"Do what?"

"Talk about what-ifs. I know I messed up. I was an idiot. It wasn't you. It was me."

"How can you say that? You left me for another woman. Of course it was me."

"It was complicated. I just got lost. I lost sight of who I was and what I wanted. I'm sorry."

They looked at each other for a long moment, tension filling the void between them. For the first time in months, she looked at Dave and saw… just Dave. The man she'd fallen for at that summer picnic with mutual friends. The man who'd asked her to marry him in the hallway of their high school because that was where he'd first told her he'd loved her. The man who brought home flowers every Friday for the first five years of their marriage.

"I know you have to get to work, but do you want to go for a walk? Esmerelda's stroller's in the car. Thought it might be nice to take a look at the neighborhood. You know, for old time's sake."

She knew she should say no. She knew it was risky, being seen with him during the day.

But the words "for old time's sake" got to her. What could it hurt? After years of history, what could a fifteen-minute walk hurt? Maybe it would help her settle some unresolved feelings. Maybe they could find a middle ground to this weird state they were in.

Maybe she could put him in the past.

"Okay."

They headed out the door, Dave making his way to the stroller as Esmerelda cooed.

Annie shoved her hands in her pockets. The bite of the November air chilled her, but she knew it was probably more than just the weather preying on her now. This was ludicrous. She was being a fool.

As they started walking down the block, Dave spoke first. "I miss this."

Leaves crunched under her feet as she trudged down the sidewalk, a light breeze blowing up some dirt.

"Dave, I want you to know I'm happy. I don't regret what happened. I love Joe."

There was a pause.

"I know. I'm happy for you. But I still miss this. I wish things had gone differently. I do have regrets."

She eyed him, the man she'd once shared a bed with. He was close enough to brush against her arm, but he felt millions of miles away.

Tears came to her eyes, surprising her. The anger had dissipated this past year. She'd moved on from him, thanks to Joe.

But she realized now time didn't heal all wounds, and

it didn't make you forget who you were or who you loved. Second loves came into your life, and they reignited you. But they couldn't obliterate the first. They couldn't make you forget how your heart got to the second love, how it found it.

She hadn't let herself realize how unresolved she was. Not that she loved him. Not that she wanted him back. She'd just moved on with Joe so quickly, at least by her standards, that she hadn't let herself feel this.

She'd felt the anger. She'd felt the hurt.

But she hadn't properly felt grief for the destruction of their life together.

"I just never thought this would be us, or our life. Things were so perfect for us. Or at least I thought they were. And then it all went to shit. I just never dreamed I wouldn't be good enough for you anymore."

The confession came out strong despite the water streaming down her cheek. She'd said the thing she hadn't been able to say before.

Dave stopped, parking the stroller for a second. He turned to her in front of the hedges of a neighbor's house. He put the stroller's lock on and took her hands in his.

"You were always good enough for me, Annie. Please don't think that. You're beautiful and loving. You're amazing. I've always loved you."

"Then what happened, Dave? Why'd you leave?"

"The truth?"

She nodded, tears still streaming.

"I was a fucking idiot."

She opened her mouth to question him further, to figure out if this was an acceptable explanation.

But she didn't get the chance. Before words could come out, before she could argue, his mouth was on hers, a familiar mouth she'd known so many times before. His lips moved in just the right ways, and her stomach fluttered.

It was a familiar mouth, a familiar kiss, a familiar feeling. Yet, it was also new in every way. The Dave kissing her now was simultaneously familiar and exotic, old and brand new. There was an electricity pulsating from the surprise of the encounter, from the sheer excitement of the unexpected. She felt herself give in to the kiss, her heart overpowering her head, her memories guiding her lips in the conquest of this moment.

And then a horn honked, and she snapped out of it. She peeked around Dave, trying to figure out what was happening.

Mouth open and rage quickly flooding his face, Joe stared through the window of his truck at her, hand paused over the horn. His gaze locked with Annie's, now stupefied, before he slammed on the gas and peeled out of the neighborhood.

"Shit!" Annie cried, tears now flowing even more.

Dave, also stupefied, looked from the truck to Annie.

"Looks like I'm a fucking idiot again."

"That makes two of us." Annie dashed down the street, away from Dave and the past-slash-future that would never be. Her feet pounded the pavement as she headed back to the house she shared with her new husband, the husband she hoped was still hers.

***

How did I get here? Annie thought as she continued pacing through the house. She heard the sound of an engine, and for the fifth time in the past hour, she dashed to the front window, hoping it was him but also wondering what she would say if it was.

She'd expected him to be standing in the living room or sitting at the kitchen island, waiting to work this out. She knew he'd be pissed, and rightfully so, but her naiveté had assured her he'd be here. Joe would always be here. She'd messed up, but she would set it straight.

When she'd dashed into the house, though, heart fluttering from her impromptu run home and the situation itself, she'd found an empty house. A cold, empty house that suddenly shrieked at her, underscoring the bleakness that would now be hers.

And it was all her fault.

Sure, Dave had been the one to kiss her. She'd been swept up in the momentum of their talk, of the tangled web of their past. But she hadn't stopped him.

She hadn't stopped him when he first came to the door with Esmerelda. She hadn't stopped him when he kept coming around. She hadn't stopped sneaking around behind Joe's back.

Now, everything was a mess.

She'd already called Macy, apologizing profusely for having to call off completely. Her boss had said she'd understood. She couldn't possibly, though. She'd tried to call Joe, but she kept getting sent straight to voice mail. There was nothing to do but wallow and wait.

Annie wrapped herself in a sweatshirt and sank into the sofa, tears flowing down her cheeks. She needed to talk to Joe, to apologize, to make him understand. But how could she? What could she possibly say to make him understand? Did she even understand herself?

Maybe she'd been a fool to think second loves could, in fact, work out. Maybe she'd been a fool to think love itself could work out.

As she combed over every question, though, another engine hummed outside, this one familiar. She heard the garage door open and then, a few minutes later, she heard it close. She heard the tromping boots and the opening of the door leading from the garage.

She leaped from the couch, arms wrapped around herself. He stood at the doorway, staring at her. Gone was the look of love and softness. Gone was the familiarity in his gaze, the warmth in his expression. In its place were feelings all too familiar to Annie—hurt, fear, and rejection.

"Joe," she started, but stopped when he shook his head.

"I can't, Annie. I can't do this." He dashed up the stairs, turning his back on her. Desperation creeping in, she followed.

"Joe, *please*. Just listen." She followed him into their bedroom. He kneeled in their closet, rifling through for his duffle bag. The action said it all, piercing Annie's heart.

He tossed the duffle on the bed and started grabbing things from his dresser drawers, flinging random articles of clothing into the bag.

"What is there to say, Annie?"

"Joe, I'm sorry. It wasn't what it looked like."

"It wasn't what it looked like? Really? Because to me, it looked a hell of a lot like you kissing your ex-husband. It looked to me like you were feeling pretty cozy, pretty close with the man you used to be married to. It looked a whole lot like my wife was sneaking around behind my back with a man she loves."

"Joe… I… I don't love him. I'm sorry. I didn't mean for it to happen." She wrapped herself tighter in the sweatshirt, the rage in his gaze chilling her. Tears streamed down her face, soaking into her shirt. Breathing was difficult, her throat tight from tears and devastation. He was already gone, a series of bad choices distancing her from the man she truly loved.

"Save it, Annie. I love you. I knew going into this it was complicated. I knew it wasn't going to be easy for you to move on, and I respect that. I can't know what it's been like for you. I've been patient. But I will not be married to a woman whose heart belongs to another man. I can't do this, love or not."

She reached for his arm, hoping to pull him back, but he shook her off. It scared her to see him this angry. It was the antithesis of who Joe was.

She'd done this to him. She'd ruined what they had. She'd risked the true love of her life, the man who meant everything to her, and for what? A kiss with a man who was her past? A few moments of connection based on nostalgia?

"Joe, please believe me. I love you."

Joe grabbed his duffle bag from the bed, slinging it over a shoulder. He turned to look at Annie, who was standing in the middle of the bedroom.

"That's what makes this so hard, Annie. Because for a while there, I actually believed you."

She clutched her chest, sobs racking her frame now at the gravity of his words. He gave her one last sorrowful glance. He looked like he was going to reach out to her, to touch her, but then he seemed to change his mind. He turned and smoothly walked out the bedroom door. She heard his boots on the steps. She heard him pause at the landing before opening the front door and slamming it behind him.

Annie crumpled to the floor, a heap of tears, snot, guilt, and regrets as she heard the engine of his truck roar to life before Joe left her, their home, and most likely their love behind.

Chapter Thirteen

Charlotte

"Dear, I think that's wonderful. You're going to have such a great time," Charlotte proclaimed as she plunked her spoon into her mashed potatoes.

"Yeah, I think it'll be good for us to just go out." Amelia prepared to cut her meatloaf with her fork and knife. The girl hated meatloaf. Perhaps it was a sign of the baby growing; her cravings were beginning.

They were at the usual haunt, enjoying a quiet lunch together. It had been a while since Charlotte and Amelia had time like this, with Amelia working her three jobs again and Charlotte wrapped up in several volunteer groups at Wildflower. It seemed like every year, their lives just got busier and busier. Soon, the presence of a little one would amplify their hectic schedules even more.

Charlotte couldn't wait to hold her great-grandbaby.

"Well, you two should enjoy it now. Pretty soon, things are about to get even crazier," Charlotte said between bites of food.

Amelia got a despondent look in her eye. Charlotte put her silverware down, reaching across the table for her granddaughter's hand.

"Chin up, honey. It's going to be fine."

"I know. I think. It's just not what we had planned."

"Dear, we've been through this. Life is never as we plan. It's going to be okay. You've got a great man beside you."

"Yeah, a great man who gave everything up. For me."

"Well, you're worth it. Seriously. Stop beating yourself up over this. Owen knew what he was getting himself into when you two… well… you know."

"Grandma!"

"I'm just saying." Charlotte threw her hands in the air in defense of her words. "He's not an innocent, naïve boy. He knew what he was getting himself into. And you know what? I think he wanted to get himself into it. Because he loves you. He's crazy about you. The fact he gave up the band isn't something you should be ashamed of. You should feel secure in his love for you because of it. He *loves* you. Enough said."

They resumed eating for a few minutes before

Charlotte asked, "How's work, honey? I do worry about you and the baby. It's not good for you to work so much."

"Grandma, it's not the 1920s. I'm not even that pregnant yet. It's fine. I love my jobs. I actually realized how much I missed them, crazy as it sounds."

"Are you still writing?"

Amelia nodded. "Yeah, I'm still writing. The band still needs songs, so Owen's set up a system where I can still write music for them. It just won't be Owen singing them."

"Wonderful, darling. See, compromise. There's always a compromise. Owen will figure out one for himself too."

"Speaking of compromise, have you heard anything more from Mom about her and Joe?"

"She's been elusive about it. I thought maybe you would be able to pry more out of her."

"No, she's been top secret about it. All I know is Joe is staying at the Hampton Inn right now."

"I told her this was going to be a disaster."

"You what? You know what happened? What disaster?"

"Oh dear. You don't know?"

"No, Grandma. I told you, Mom's been real secretive. As soon as I bring up her and Joe or try to ask why she's so upset or why he's moved out for right now, she just says it's complicated and turns the subject to me. What happened?"

Charlotte shook her head, avoiding eye contact.

"You're not going to like it."

"Tell me."

"Amelia, listen. You have enough on your plate. I don't want you getting upset."

"I'm going to be upset if you don't tell me."

"Joe caught your mother kissing your father."

Amelia froze, her knife clattering to her plate. "What? Come again?"

"Joe caught your mother kissing your father."

"Grandma, I heard you. But that doesn't make any sense."

"I know. I told your mom that when she was seeing Dave."

"What? Seeing him? What are you talking about?"

Charlotte slowly revealed the whole sordid story, from the clandestine meetings between Annie and Dave to the kiss Joe had seen.

"What the hell was she thinking?"

"She clearly wasn't, dear."

Amelia braced herself on the table, her face glowing red with anger. "I can't believe this."

"I know. I just think your mom never quite sorted through everything. She was in such a hurry to put your father behind her, she didn't stop to think it might take some time to do that."

"No. This is outrageous. She loves Joe."

"Of course she does."

"Then why the hell would she kiss Dad? After what he did?"

Charlotte looked at Amelia, a feeble smile creeping onto her face. "Love's messy. You know that. I know that. We've all learned that this past year. It's complicated. There isn't a right or wrong answer. Sometimes it just is."

"Grandma, stop trying to make this sound sensible."

"Nothing about it is sensible, Amelia. But then again, nothing about life really is. We just do the best we can with the choices we have and the choices we make. That's all we can do."

"Well, Mom certainly made a messed-up choice this time."

"Yeah, I suppose you're right."

"So what do we do about this?"

"We sit back and let her figure it out. And hope everyone comes to their senses."

"And if they don't? If their love falls apart?"

"Well, then we hope they figure out where love went and find it again. Because I think your Mom and Joe belong together."

"Yeah. But sometimes belonging together doesn't guarantee love won't disappear."

Charlotte nodded before turning her attention back to her food, which had looked delicious a few minutes ago but was suddenly cold and uninviting.

Chapter Fourteen

Charlotte

"You. We need to talk right now."

Charlotte didn't have to look behind her to know whose voice was making demands. Bridget and Marla were across from Charlotte in the book club's discussion circle. The scowls on their faces said it all.

Exhaling, Charlotte got out of her folding chair and set her book down. She stood facing Catherine, who was wearing what appeared to be a red pleather mini-skirt with a lacy black halter top. There was a lot of saggy skin up for show, to Charlotte's horror.

"Can't you see we're busy right now? How dare you burst in here during book club. We were in the middle of a lovely discussion."

"Book club? You mean cookie club?" Catherine scoffed, eying the table of snacks beside the women.

"What we do here is none of your concern. There's a sign-up sheet on the bulletin board which clearly states the community room is reserved the second Tuesday of every month for the book club. So unless you signed up and brought your book, you can just leave."

"It's a free country last I checked. Besides, who would want to come talk with you old coots about some boring literature? What *are* you reading, anyway?" Catherine picked up Charlotte's book from the chair. Charlotte grabbed it from her, the two wrestling in a moment that reminded Charlotte of the Cracker Jack incident. Charlotte, to her delight, was able to rip the book from Catherine's hands.

"Don't touch my stuff. This is a signed copy."

Catherine peered at the title, forcefully turning Charlotte's hands to better see it. "Please tell me you're not reading this."

"Well, Catherine, we wouldn't expect you to understand the subject matter. Or how to read, for that matter. Now get your bingo-wing out of my face."

"*Fifty Shades of Grey*? Are you serious? What could *you* possibly know about the subject matter? Shall I start calling Leonard 'Christian'?" Catherine was laughing her polite little chuckle, the one Charlotte always wanted to smack off her face.

"Okay, enough. For your information, we were having

an enlightened book club discussion until you strutted in here in your 'fifty shades of ugly' skirt. Is that pleather?" Charlotte reached out to touch Catherine's skirt, hoping it would leave a hideous, smudgy fingerprint on the plastic material.

Catherine slapped her hand.

"It's designer."

"Of course it is," Charlotte retorted, rolling her eyes.

The book club ladies all just stared, mouths open. In fairness, there were only four of them, and one probably couldn't hear a thing they were saying. Still, at least things were definitely staying interesting. Between the Christian Grey talk and the Catherine catfight, perhaps they'd be getting more book club members when word got around.

"Anyway, I didn't come here to discuss your smutty literature with you. I came to discuss the situation unfolding with your slutty daughter."

Gasps ensued. Charlotte put a hand on her hip, reminding herself to stay calm. "Excuse me?"

Catherine strolled past Charlotte to the snack table, pawing through the cookie tray until she found a peanut butter one. Charlotte didn't take her eyes off her.

Catherine bit into the cookie and dramatically spit her bite on the floor, almost hitting Bridget with some crumbs. "This is the nastiest cookie I've ever tasted. Good thing you don't have anyone important in the book club."

"Forget the cookie. What did you say about my

daughter?" Charlotte inched toward Catherine.

"I said we need to discuss your slutty daughter. I will have you know that my son will not stand for her disgusting behavior. It's over. I'm not sure why he's so surprised by what she did. I mean, you've got to consider the influence she had in her life." Catherine struck her typical pose, arms crossed.

Charlotte, still holding her book club book, stomped toward Catherine. "Take it back."

"Take what back? The truth? Your daughter is a lying, manipulative little skank. My son is too good for her. Not that this is a surprise. I told him when they first met she couldn't be trusted. And now she proved it. I'll make sure he gets a top-notch divorce lawyer, so you better tell your daughter to be prepared. If she can stay out of her ex's bed long enough, that is."

And that's when Charlotte lost it.

Later, she would swear the book just flew out of her hands, the result of a wild, angry arm flail. Regardless, *Fifty Shades of Grey* sailed through the air, conking Catherine directly in the head.

Catherine let out a shriek even Marla heard as she stumbled backward, right into the refreshments table.

Charlotte should have apologized, should have helped her up. Maybe then the book club fiasco could've been labeled a misunderstanding, an accident.

But she didn't. Because all she heard were the words "slutty" and "skank" floating in her head in Catherine's signature condescending tone.

So Charlotte did what any sensible eightysomething would do.

She leaped onto the ground, knees on either side of Catherine's skinny frame, now drenched in red fruit punch from the table. Catherine was flailing and rolling, chucking cookies at Charlotte's head. The book club women leaped from their chairs—as fast as eightysomethings can leap, that is—and formed a new circle around the women.

"Get her, Charlotte," Bridget yelled, fist pumping near Catherine's head.

"You selfish, pleather-wearing witch," Charlotte screamed.

"Ladies!"

Charlotte and Catherine froze, both covered in sticky punch and cookies. Charlotte also didn't need to turn to identify the voice screaming or the heels clicking on the floor.

She felt a hand firmly pulling her to her feet.

She turned to see Cassie, hair frizzed, eyes raging.

"What in the hell is going on here?"

The book club women gasped. Chipper Cassie rarely swore. This must be serious.

"Oh, they were just reenacting a scene from the book we're reading," Bridget chimed in. Catherine, now on her feet and brushing crumbs off her skirt in horror, turned to Bridget.

"What scene would that be? Because I don't remember there being a scene with two elderly ladies killing each other in that book. But then again, maybe I just don't remember it," Cassie announced.

Everyone stood silent for a moment.

"You know you owe me a new skirt now. And this wasn't cheap. It'll cost you nine hundred dollars," Catherine said, glaring at Charlotte.

"And you owe us reimbursement for our refreshments and the cost of books since we didn't get to fully discuss it."

"You wish. This is your fault anyway for raising such a—"

"Enough!" Cassie screamed, actually clutching at her hair as if she were going to rip it out. She started counting out loud. Charlotte thought they might have done it, that she might completely snap.

"Listen. I'm going to go back to my office to do some of the stacks of paperwork I have to complete. You two are going to clean up the mess on the floor. Charlotte, you're going to dismiss the book club's meeting for the month. You're all going to say that book club was super uneventful today, rather dull actually. In fact, it was so dull, there are no longer any members of the club. There are no longer book club meetings at all. No one likes reading anyway, right?"

Charlotte opened her mouth to challenge Cassie, to argue it wasn't fair.

But the look in Cassie's eyes said it all. Charlotte actually took a step back, nodding.

She wasn't afraid of a snobby eightysomething in a

hideously revealing skirt. She wasn't afraid to get dirty, to get coated in cookies and punch for a good cause.

She wasn't, however, stupid enough to fight with a thirtysomething who truly looked like she was at her breaking point. She'd watched enough *Dateline* to know the look of someone ready to snap. Fruit punch could be cleaned up—blood was a different story.

So Charlotte nodded as Catherine smirked, nose in the air. Cassie spun on her heels and stomped back to her office.

"You'll pay for this," Charlotte articulated through gritted teeth, tossing a leftover cookie at Catherine before Catherine, too, spun on her heels and stomped out. She stopped at the door to turn and wink at Charlotte.

"Thanks for the cookies and the lovely discussion. I'm so glad I stopped by for the final book club meeting. It's a shame you just can't keep membership up." With a laugh, she was gone.

Oh yes, Charlotte thought. *That woman definitely has to pay.*

Chapter Fifteen

Amelia

Amelia folded the last towel, shoving it on the pile in the laundry basket before dragging the basket to the bedroom.

It was somewhat comforting to be back in a routine, doing normal things. It was also somewhat unnerving, though. Domestic life was quite a bit different from the tour life. Folding towels wasn't quite as exciting as booking gigs or sightseeing, but it was home. Life was changing. That wasn't necessarily a bad thing.

As she walked into the bedroom, she found Owen sitting cross-legged on their bed. He was wearing his boxers and a plain T-shirt, a few suitcases in front of him.

"What are you doing?" she asked, leaning in to kiss him and then deciding to join him.

"Hey, baby. Just finally sorting through some stuff. Trying to get settled back in."

She nodded, understanding exactly what he'd meant. It was so strange because not long ago, this had been home. But now, it was like readjusting to an alien world. Settling back in was surprisingly difficult, finding a place for everything again. Sorting through belongings, sorting through life.

With the baby on the way, they also had space constraints to think about. At Owen's insistence, they'd already started mapping out layouts in the apartment, trying to figure out how everything was going to mesh together until they could save for a bigger apartment.

Owen was pawing through the suitcase, pulling out random items that had been with them on the road. Amelia started going through the second one, helping him to sort out the remnants of a life now ending before it had even matured.

True to Owen's style, nothing was organized. Amelia pulled out CDs, a leather belt, a T-shirt, and a favorite coffee mug.

"Does it hurt?"

Owen stopped unpacking, looking at her. "What?"

"This. Unpacking. Backtracking."

He laced his fingers in hers. "Stop. I'm not backtracking. I'm right where I'm supposed to be."

Amelia leaned against his shoulder. "I love you. But

it has to be weird. Not long ago, you were packing these suitcases to take with you on the road. And now here you are, getting ready to go back to Wildflower tomorrow."

"Shh. Stop. We've been through this. I love you. I love this life. I'm excited to take this journey with you. Sure, it might not be the journey we envisioned when we packed months ago. But it's our journey. And that's all that matters."

She grinned, feeling joy radiating through her veins as he leaned her back on the bed, kissing her in that familiar way she'd come to crave.

Later, though, when their passion had been quenched, the towels had been put away, and the bags unpacked, she stumbled across him in the living room. He was staring at a photograph on the wall.

The photograph was of Owen with his bandmates at their first gig.

She didn't say anything, didn't interrupt him. His stance, the expression on his face when he turned away, though, said it all.

He might be excited to take this journey with her, but he was definitely mourning the loss of another journey— the journey he wasn't going to get to take.

Chapter Sixteen

Amelia

"Are you expecting someone?" Amelia asked. Owen turned from washing their dinner dishes.

"No."

"Maybe it's Mom or Grandma."

"Your mom or grandma knocking? Really?" Owen grinned.

"You're right."

She walked to the door, peeking out the hole to see who it was. She froze.

"No freaking way," she mumbled. *What in the hell is he doing here?*

Owen turned off the faucet and came up behind her.

"Amelia?"

Amelia ignored him, though, flinging open the door. She didn't even try to hide her rage. "What are *you* doing here?"

Her father, hands in his pockets, fidgeted with loose change. "Um, I'm so sorry to bother you, especially without calling."

"What do you want?" Amelia asked again, showing every bit of hurt in the tone of her voice.

"I just…. I'm worried. I can't reach your mother, and I wanted to see if everything was okay."

Amelia laughed in exasperation. "Are you serious right now?" She shook her head, taking a step toward her father. "You manipulate your way back into her life and then fuck up her new relationship, and you want information? You want to know if she's okay? No, she isn't. What, couldn't you stand the fact she might be able to move on from you? So you felt the need to mess up her life a second time? Unbelievable." Amelia, still shaking her head, turned to head back into the apartment.

"Amelia, just, please, hear me out."

Disgust boiled in her chest. She reminded herself to breathe, reminded herself not to scream like a crazy person. Owen held the door open now, eying Amelia with confusion and concern. Amelia leaned against him, looking her father dead in the eye.

"You want to help Mom? You want to make things better? Stay out of our lives. For good."

Her father stood for a moment, staring at the two

of them. He started to say something, but seemed to change his mind, perhaps deciding it was futile. The hurt expression on her dad's face, the softness of his steps as he walked away, and the silence as he disappeared drifted in the stale air of the hallway. Amelia told herself it served him right, told herself this was outrageous.

But when the hallway was empty and Owen slowly shut the door, she felt the tears welling up. She felt the pain and the anger dissipate into a strange sense of bleak despair.

Owen wrapped her in his arms, rocking her slowly.

"I don't even know why I'm crying. This is ridiculous," she said, wiping away the tears. Owen gently pulled her hands away from her face.

"You're crying because, no matter what, he's your dad. He's family, Amelia. And you might hate him for what he did, you might not agree with him, but he will always be your dad. So cry. Let yourself feel everything you've kept locked up."

Amelia wanted to argue, to say he really wasn't her father anymore, not in her book. The stubbornness in her floated to the surface, convincing her she'd done the right thing by shoving him out of her life. She'd done the right thing by telling him to leave. She didn't need him, not after what he'd done.

"I know things are touchy right now, but your mom and Joe will work it out. And when they do, when things smooth over, you know your mom won't blame you if you want to keep your dad in your life."

"I wouldn't do that to her."

"Listen," Owen said, brushing a strand of hair from her face. "Your mom will get it. He's your dad. Yeah, he's a dumbass. Yeah, he was a jerk to your mom. But he's *your dad*. He helped make you who you are. Whether you want to admit it to yourself or not, I think you know that. I think you know it's important to figure out how to make things right with him. This distance between you has gone on long enough. It's not good for you or the baby."

Looking at Owen, she realized this man knew her better than she knew herself. He saw things in her, saw her vulnerabilities and her flaws. Instead of running from them, though, he helped her run at them, making her better as he helped her sort out the messy things in her life.

"I'm not ready to forgive him yet," she whispered, a truth she hadn't spoken out loud.

"It's okay. It'll take time. You'll get there."

She wasn't sure if he was right, wasn't sure how much time it would take. She wasn't sure if she could forgive her father or even if she wanted to.

But she did know that Owen was exactly the man she needed in her life, exactly the kind of man who would make a great father to their baby. She knew he'd never be the kind of man their child would want to push away. He'd never be Amelia's father.

She wrapped her arms around his neck and leaned in, hugging him tighter, realizing how lucky she was in spite of everything.

Chapter Seventeen

Annie

Somehow, she managed to survive it.

She'd painted on a huge, toothy grin when Mrs. Adamson insisted her anniversary party needed to be an *Alice in Wonderland* theme, including a Cheshire cat piñata. She'd consoled a twenty-year-old bridezilla who was certain the pink in the linen sample Annie showed her would clash terribly with the pink in her bridesmaids' dresses. She'd written a to-do list with exactly forty-seven items to be completed for the Corles's birthday bash for their daughter next weekend. She'd pretended to care about all the trivial party fiascos that came up. She'd shown up for work, got the job done, and managed to make Macy believe she was actually competent.

But the whole time, through the bridezilla tears and the bossy clients, her mind was miles away. Her mind had her standing by that stroller in the middle of that kiss when everything changed. Her mind was miles away at the Hampton Inn, wondering what Joe was doing or thinking. Her mind was miles away at the tacky altar, remembering the vows she'd made to Joe when he vowed to love her forever.

For the past few nights, she'd given in to old habits. She'd grabbed some takeout and planted herself on the couch. She'd attempted to drown her sorrows in soap operas and fried chicken, numbing her mind with glass after glass of wine.

Tonight, though, the thought of the emptiness of the house chilled her. She'd lived alone for months after Dave left, but suddenly, without Joe there, her echoing footsteps were more noticeable. The empty side of the bed, the sight of his vacant chair at breakfast, the silence other than the cats' cries—it all blared in her brain with incessant, biting clarity. He was gone. She was alone. She'd lost him.

She wasn't ready to face it all, so she turned right at the stop sign instead of left, passing familiar sights in the town. She passed the school where she'd once been a bright-eyed teenager ready to take on life, love, and the entire world. She passed the park down the street where Amelia used to beg her to push her just one more time on the swings. She passed the familiar ice-cream stand Joe stopped at every Friday night on his way home from work to grab her favorite pint. She passed the pizza shop where she and Dave used to go after football games during high school. She passed the skating rink complex where Joe would clutch her arm, promising not to let her fall.

The memories of two lives taunted her, and the tears started to fall. Everything was such a mess, as usual. Nothing could ever just be simple in her life.

Before she knew it, the tears were slowly clearing and she found herself at a familiar place, a place she hadn't really thought she was going. A place she subconsciously needed to be, apparently.

She slowly unbuckled her seat belt and crawled from the seat, not caring that her mascara was probably clumping and streaking or that her face was most likely blotchy. She ambled toward the familiar area, the bench forever engrained in her mind as the place she'd started over.

She took a seat on the bench where her second chance had started, where a kiss had incited a beautiful journey instead of one of sadness. Sitting there, she closed her eyes. She could picture it like it was yesterday. The joy of a new beginning, the rush of feeling things she thought her heart had forever cordoned off. She felt the warmth, the safety of Joe's arms, the tender touch of his hands on her cheek. She heard the promise whispered between their hearts in that moment that this was something magical, something that could reawaken both of them to life and love.

She kept her eyes closed as tears started to stream again, the pain behind them searing her skin and her heart. Her head ached from her grief. Her heart ached from her guilt. What had she been thinking? How could she do this to Joe? How could she risk the best thing that had happened to her for a man who had hurt her so badly?

At the sound of footsteps, she jolted back to the present, her eyes popping open to see a familiar face. She hurriedly wiped away tears, painting on the smile she'd grown accustomed to wearing.

Charlotte sat down beside Annie, patting her knee with her cold, aging hand.

"You don't have to wipe away your tears for me. You're not fooling anyone."

Annie sighed. "You were right, Mom."

"Of course I was, dear. Haven't you learned by now I'm always right?"

Annie turned to glare at Charlotte, but Charlotte's wink made her smile. Annie leaned down, propping her elbows on her knees, burying her head in her hands. "I've messed everything up, Mom. Everything. Joe's not coming back."

Charlotte wrapped an arm around Annie's shoulders like she had so many times in Annie's life. Annie let herself lean against Charlotte, the coldness of her mother's skin nullified by the warm feeling of safety and comfort rising up from the depths of Annie.

"There, there. It's going to be fine. It's always fine."

"Not this time. Joe hasn't come home. He's never going to forgive me."

"Of course he will."

Annie pulled back. "Why should he? I hurt him."

"Yeah, you did. But he'll forgive you. He loves you. And sometimes love just hurts. That doesn't mean you throw in the towel."

"But what if he has?"

"Then you hand the towel to him. You remind him you're worth fighting for."

"Maybe I'm not."

Charlotte slapped Annie's shoulder.

"Ow. What the heck was that for?"

"For being ridiculous. Now, yes, things are bad right now. But I will not sit here and let you throw yourself a pity party. Stop it. Get it together, Annie. Do you love Joe?"

"Yes."

"I hate to even spit this question out, but do you love Dave?"

"Of course not."

"Thank goodness. Because if you'd said 'yes,' I think I would have put you in a headlock until you changed your mind."

"I don't doubt that for a second."

"So things are simple. You love Joe. You don't love Dave. You just need to show him. You need to fight for him, Annie."

"And how do I do that? He won't even speak to me. He hasn't come home."

"Then you go get him. Go to him and make him listen to you. Love is never easy, and it's never promised. Your father and I had plenty of moments when I thought it was over. But we fixed it. You know why? Because we loved each other. We believed we were worth it. You need to believe that too."

Annie took a few deep breaths, her mother's words sinking in. She ruffled her hair with her hand, her gaze steadying, her resolve coming into focus.

"You're right. I can't just wait for things to patch themselves up. I need to make him understand." Annie hugged Charlotte. "Thanks, Mom. Love you."

"You're welcome, honey."

Annie sprung from the bench, readjusting her shirt and heading toward her car.

"Annie?" Charlotte called, and Annie turned around.

"What, Mom?"

"For the love of God, you're not going to win any man back with mascara smudges like that. Fix your face before you go. It looks terrible. You have to put your best foot forward. Use your womanly charm."

Annie grinned, shaking her head. "Okay, Mom. Got it."

"I know you do," she said. "Oh, and 513."

"What?" Annie asked.

"He's in room 513 at the Hampton Inn."

Annie scrunched her eyebrows together. "How do

you know that?"

"Well, you see—"

Annie tossed her hands up. "You know, on second thought, I probably don't want to know. I've got to go. I'll call you."

Annie rushed to her car, her new mission in sight. She pulled out of Wildflower determined that the second-chance kiss at the Wildflower bench wouldn't be for nothing.

Chapter Eighteen

Annie

Nervousness filled Annie's chest, stomach, and head. What if this was a terrible idea? What if Joe still needed space? What would she say once she made it into the room? What if he asked for a divorce?

The questions almost made her back down, change her mind, and run out of the Hampton Inn, but she'd already stomped up five flights of stairs—the elevator was taking too long. She was winded and her calves hurt. She was going to make this count for something.

She pounded on the door a second time, glancing at her watch. Joe should be back from work by now. She put an ear to the door, hearing what sounded like the muffled sound of water.

Exasperated and impatient, she glanced down the hallway. A maid was pushing a cleaning cart, probably more than ready to head home for the day, based on the exhausted look on her face.

"Excuse me, ma'am," Annie yelled. The maid didn't look up.

"Ma'am?" Annie called out again, this time heading toward her. When she finally got to the cart—the maid had simply frozen in place, probably hoping Annie wasn't going to ask her something complicated—she started talking a mile a minute, her nerves getting to her again.

"Hi, I'm sorry to bother you, but I forgot my room key and my husband is in the shower. Is there any way you can just open the door for me? Do you have a key?"

The maid scratched her super smooth, super tight librarian bun. "It's against policy."

"Please. Just this once? It'll be our little secret."

"I can't. Sorry."

"Look, please. Just this once. I don't want to have to go the whole way downstairs and I just really, really am having a bad day, and…."

The maid glanced at her watch. "Fine. Whatever. I put in my two-week notice this morning, so I guess it doesn't really matter anyway."

"Thank you so much!" Annie practically skipped down the hallway, the maid trudging along behind her. When they finally got to the door and the maid swiped her card, Annie thanked her a few more times before walking into the room.

She probably should've just been patient and waited a few more minutes. It didn't matter. She was here now. She leaned back against the door to the room, taking a deep breath, preparing herself for the speech to come. She heard the shower turn off.

She was nervous. She couldn't wait another minute. She softly walked toward the bathroom.

"Joe?" she said, peeking around the corner to where the shower was, the bathroom door ajar. Her jaw dropped when her eyes landed on the figure standing by the shower.

It took a moment for her brain to realize the six-pack abs, the tan skin—none of it belonged to Joe.

"*What the?!*" the male voice bellowed as Annie jumped back into the bedroom area, her eyes wide and her heart stopping. She threw her hands up in front of her face in defense as the man in the bathroom stumbled out into the bedroom, a towel around his waist.

"Who the hell are you?" he demanded, coming closer to her as she backed away.

"I'm so sorry," she said, stumbling past the bed, trying to figure out where to look. "I thought... I was... I must've...."

"Get out, you sicko," he said.

Annie wanted to apologize again, to explain the situation. But this strange man, the towel, the compromising situation she'd met him in—it was a scene right out of a bad comedy. She couldn't think of what would be an appropriate reply, so she just scrambled to the door and shut it behind her. She dashed for the stairwell, running down two flights before pausing on a landing to catch her breath.

When her heart stopped beating out of her chest, she continued down the steps. She was really going to hurt her mother, eightysomething or not, when she got hold of her. This was all her fault. Hopefully that man was simply a tourist. God forbid if she ran into him in the grocery store or something.

She still felt like she wanted to die from embarrassment, but more than that, she was frustrated. She needed to get to Joe. This time, she would ask for the correct room number, like she should've done all along.

When she arrived at the front desk, though, and asked for Joe's room number, her heart plummeted again.

Joe had checked out late that afternoon. He was gone.

***

Certain that Joe's departure from the Hampton Inn was the final sign of doomsday for their relationship, Annie did what any self-respecting woman in her position would do.

She went to her fallback plan, grabbing some greasy fried chicken from a drive-thru and a fresh bottle of wine at the liquor store. Trudging from her car with none of her dignity left and all of her comfort items, she wriggled open the door. Butternut and Peter greeted her, meowing for the fried food they'd grown accustomed to in the past few nights. The sight of them just reminded her of what she had to look forward to—a true, crazy cat lady life.

Sighing and plopping her purchases on the counter, she kicked off her heels and started heading for the stairs to change into her at-home uniform of yoga pants. She paused, though, before she ascended past the first step. There was a light on down the hall in the guest bedroom. She never even went in that room, so she certainly hadn't left a light on.

She felt her heart flutter with hope, a brief glimpse of the truest but slimmest wish in her heart. Hoping she wasn't walking into the trap of a serial killer, she inched her way along the hallway.

The cats' cries behind her didn't really do much for the sneaking part. When she peered in the guest bedroom door, relief of all varieties flooded her.

It wasn't a serial killer; it was Joe. He wasn't gone.

He turned from the window he was staring out. He had several days of stubble on his face, and his flannel shirt was wrinkled. He looked disheveled, a bit worn, but he looked a lot more like the Joe she remembered than the Joe who had stormed out of their home, out of her life.

"Hey," she said. It was a simple word, but she didn't really know what else to say. She hated the tension in the room. It was stifling yet icy. It felt so unnatural, especially with this man in whom she'd found such comfort.

"Hey," he said back. They stood, frozen in the web of complexities that had woven itself between them. Annie wanted nothing more than to run into his arms, to beg for forgiveness, to feel their love repairing itself.

"I'm glad to see you. I'm glad you're home."

"Where were you? I got home a while ago, but you weren't here."

"I was out looking for you. I actually went to the hotel to talk to you, but you were gone."

He stared, no response forming on his lips. Annie looked at him, the man who, up until a few days ago, shared her bed, knew her biggest fears. He knew when she was frightened, could sense when she needed support. Now, though, he looked at her like he didn't know her at all. His eyes were filled with suspicion.

"It's pretty late. You got off work a while ago." His hands were in his pockets, arms rigid. He stood tall, perhaps trying to strike his most intimidating stance.

"I was driving around first. I went to see Mom for a while."

He nodded, but she knew this wasn't the answer he had set in his mind. His eyes were questioning, and she knew what he was wondering even if he wasn't brave enough to ask.

"Damn it, I hate this," she said through an exhale. "I hate what I've done to us."

"Me too."

"Joe, I love you. That kiss with Dave meant nothing. Absolutely nothing."

He dropped his hands from his pockets, his gestures now punctuating his pent-up anger as he talked. "How can you say that? How can you say it meant nothing? Because to me, Annie, it meant a hell of a lot. It meant you're not over him. It meant you were lying to me, sneaking behind my back. And more importantly, it meant that maybe this isn't what you actually want."

"You know that isn't true."

"Do I? Because I thought so. I knew there would always be something between you. I'm not an idiot. But I thought our love was real enough to make you want to move on. I thought you wanted us. Imagine my surprise to find out I was wrong."

Tears started flowing again, the familiar foe from the past few days. The pain resurged, and the hopes of an amicable reunion, of undeserved but craved forgiveness, waned.

"I'm sorry. I know I've hurt you. But I do want this. I want *you*. I love you."

"I just don't know, Annie. I don't know if I can trust that."

His words hurt worse than if he'd slapped her. This was what it boiled down to. She'd done that to them. He didn't trust her anymore. And without trust, what hope did they have?

"I understand," she said, sinking down to the guest room bed. "I know I messed up. But I love you. Can't we try to work past this? I'll do anything."

He clenched his jaw, apparently lost in thought. "I'm here, aren't I?"

She nodded feebly. It was a step, but a small step. He

was in the guest room. His choice said a lot.

"Look, I'm not over this, Annie, not even close. I still have a lot to sort through and a lot of questions. I'm not ready to just move on. But I'm here. It's a start. I need time, though."

Time. She could live with that. It *was* a start.

"Okay."

"Okay."

She waited for him to make a move, to show a sign they were on the right path. She needed to feel his arms around her, and she selfishly wished he could let it go.

But he didn't. Maybe he couldn't. He just turned back to the window, and she took it as her cue to leave. Wringing her hands, she quietly stood up and plodded out of the room. She changed into her yoga pants, which suddenly seemed sad instead of comfy. She returned to her fried chicken, now cold, and the comfort of the couch cushions, her salty tears reminding her in many ways, she was still alone.

Chapter Nineteen

Charlotte

Maybe I should do more dance aerobics or join the strength training circuit on Wednesdays, Charlotte thought as she heaved the final bag onto the stack in front of the door. She looked over her shoulder for the third time. The coast was clear.

Not that Catherine would have any doubt in her mind as to who had done it. The important thing, though, was she wouldn't have any proof. No witnesses meant she didn't have a varicose-veined leg to stand on.

Giving the stack of bird seed a final pat, she tiptoed back down the hallway to her apartment. She wiped her brow and tried to calm her breathing. Leonard would be back from chess club any minute. She'd had a rough enough time explaining why she was heading to the store without him, let alone hauling the bags of parakeet seed into Wildflower without getting caught. Her shoulders were aching, but she smiled knowing her plan was in place.

Catherine could go ahead and strut around the community room bragging about the disintegration of the book club. Pretty soon little Marilyn would also be disintegrating right in front of Catherine's eyes.

Oh sure, Catherine would try to retaliate, would try to get Horace taken away, but Charlotte wasn't worried. She could sweet-talk her way out of trouble with Cassie, and she could always hide him with Bridget.

She knew Leonard wouldn't approve of the war starting up again, but she couldn't just sit and do nothing. Catherine was stirring the pot with Annie and Joe. She was poisoning him against Annie. Things were tough enough. Charlotte wouldn't let the crazy woman add to the chaos.

After taking a quick shower and changing, she heard the apartment door open.

"I'm home, honey. You ready to go out and do that shopping now?"

"Of course, dear," she said, jovially leaning toward him to give him a peck on the cheek.

"Wow, someone's in a good mood. Did you have that much fun without me?"

"Of course not. I just sort of poked around."

"I hope your poking around didn't involve taking any stabs at Catherine."

Charlotte winced. "I hate that you're always thinking the worst of me."

"And I hate that when it comes to that woman, I have to. After your ranting about the book club—"

"Oh, come on. Book club was just an excuse for us to eat cookies and drink punch. I'm over it."

Leonard raised an eyebrow, so Charlotte tried to change the subject. "Let's go. The bus to the mall leaves in fifteen minutes. I can't wait to get some baby clothes. It's been so long since I've got to go baby shopping."

"You know, we do have quite some time before the baby's here."

"Not *that* long. And I won't have my grandbaby coming into the world without a full wardrobe."

"I'm sure you won't. Between you, Catherine, Annie, and Marla, that baby better have an entire room for a closet."

"Well, knowing Catherine, she'll be trying to buy the little darling Jimmy Choos." Charlotte rolled her eyes, scoffing at the image of Catherine shoving a newborn's feet into super expensive heels.

"Jimmy what?"

"Nothing, Leonard. Come on. No more talk of Catherine. Let's go get to our bus."

Leonard nodded. Charlotte leaned down to give Horace a few treats and a kiss before they headed out the door.

On the way out the front entrance, Charlotte popped her head into Cassie's office.

"Cassie?"

"Yes, Charlotte," Cassie said, smiling. The smile was wide enough, but it certainly didn't look quite genuine.

"Catherine asked if I could let you know she needed to talk to you about next week's residents' meeting."

"And why are you letting me know? Why isn't Catherine coming down to talk to me?"

Charlotte hadn't quite thought of that. She could feel Leonard's gaze on her back, but she just waved her hand behind her to let him know to stay quiet.

"Um, well, I think she said something about having tea and cookies for you?"

"I have tea, thanks. Tell her to come down."

"I think she was just waiting for you. Listen, we have to get going. We have a bus to catch. But you should probably head over there. Wouldn't want to keep her waiting, you know?"

Cassie stared, not even trying to hide her suspicion.

Charlotte put her hands up in front of her, shaking her head. "I'm just telling you what she said."

Cassie sighed. "I'll head over in a few minutes."

"Great. Have a good afternoon," Charlotte said, smiling and waving as Leonard grabbed her arm and pulled her outside toward the bus.

"Charlotte?"

"What?"

"Don't 'what' me. You know exactly what I'm asking."

"Well, there were too many 'whats' in that sentence. Now I'm just lost. Oh look, it's the bus. We better hurry."

Leonard grabbed his forehead, exhaling. "You two will be the death of me with your incessant fighting and schemes."

"I hope not," Charlotte said, winking as she climbed the bus steps.

***

"Leonard, isn't this the most adorable thing you've ever seen?"

Charlotte held the tiny pink onesie to her face, the soft fabric warming her cheek and her heart. How could she forget how tiny babies were? How could she possibly wait to hold that grandbaby?

"It's pretty cute. But we don't know it's going to be a girl."

Charlotte scowled. "Don't ruin my fun. And besides, of course it's going to be a girl."

"How do you know? You didn't visit that fortune teller in the middle of the mall while I was in the bathroom, did you?"

Charlotte grinned. "No, of course not. I just have a feeling. Women know these things." She didn't bother telling Leonard she'd briefly considered going to Madame Kassandra's stand. She couldn't help it—the glitzy purple curtains were just so pretty.

"Well, what if you're wrong?"

Charlotte laughed. "Really?"

"Point taken. It's good to see you so excited.

Grandchildren are just such a blessing, especially the first. When you have your own kids, you think you can't possibly love another human being more than that. But when you hold that grandbaby for the first time, it's not that it's necessarily more love than you had for your kids. It's just on a whole new level."

Charlotte nudged him. "Getting all sappy on me, huh? I like it."

"Don't tell anyone. I don't want to lose my reputation for being a tough guy."

"Yeah, well Horace and I know the truth."

"Horace and I just wish you'd stop fighting with Catherine. You know, she could go to Cassie about him and then things are going to get messy."

"I'm not worried. I can take care of Catherine *and* Cassie, for that matter."

Leonard sighed. "Why can't you two just get along? You're family now, for God's sake."

"Don't remind me." Charlotte went to another rack, loading Leonard's arms with outfit after outfit.

"What about the baby? Don't you think it's going to be unhealthy for him—" Charlotte glared, so Leonard retracted his statement. "Sorry. Don't you think it's going to be unhealthy for *her* to be around all this fighting?"

"You're right. So Catherine better just simmer down."

"Just Catherine?"

"She starts it all."

"And you finish it."

Charlotte paused from flipping through the racks.

"Are you trying to make me angry during our shopping trip for the baby? The angrier I get, the more outfits I buy, you know. And the longer it'll be before we can hit the food court."

At that, Leonard grinned. "Okay, okay. I'm done. I just…. I think this family has enough going on right now. I'd think maybe we could try to smooth the waters a bit. Or at least not rock them even more."

Charlotte's shoulders slumped. "I guess you're right. I hadn't thought of it that way. But listen, things are getting better with Annie and Joe. Joe's back in the house at least. And Amelia and Owen seem to be getting used to the baby idea. I think it's all going to be okay."

"Listen, I never questioned that. Amelia and Owen are crazy in love, and so are Annie and Joe. You don't just throw a love like that out. Sure, sometimes stuff happens, but you get through."

"You're right. They're just young. They still think love is perfect."

"Not even close."

"You mean pretty close, right?" Charlotte asked pointedly.

"Of course. Exactly what I meant." He leaned over to kiss her cheek. "But you know what I mean. I'm sure you and Charlie had your moments."

"Did we ever. There were at least ten times we thought it was over."

"What got you through?"

"Same thing I'm sure got you and Lila through."

"What's that?"

"Love. The real kind. The kind that, no matter what happens, makes it worth fighting for. That's what Annie and Joe have. That's what Owen and Amelia have. Even if they can't see it yet, they will."

"Same kind of love we have, too, huh?"

"Of course. But you're not really helping your tough guy image, you know?"

Leonard held up a few of the frilly baby girl outfits. "No use fighting it at this point. Look at me. I'm a clothing rack for sparkles."

Charlotte laughed, adding a few more outfits to the stack before ushering Leonard to the cash register.

Things were messy right now, that was for sure. But the family had so many good things, so many blessings. They just had to pull through and be strong.

Chapter Twenty

Charlotte

Charlotte unloaded all the baby clothes from their bags, looking at each item again once they were back home. Horace was trying to curl up on the outfits, and Charlotte was hurriedly pushing him away.

"No, no, baby. We can't have the grandbaby developing cat allergies. That won't do."

A pounding on the door made Charlotte jump. "Leonard," she called out to the living room. "Can you get it?"

The pounding continued. *Goodness, someone's desperate,* Charlotte thought. I wonder who....

And then it came to her. She knew exactly who was at the door.

"Uh-oh, Horace. Get ready. It's showtime."

Charlotte rushed out to the kitchen area like a kid on Christmas. She tried to remain calm and collected, tried not to look too anxious.

Catherine blew through the door as soon as Leonard opened it. "What the hell, you old hag? What the hell are you trying to pull? You sneaky, manipulative old *biddy*." Catherine rushed toward her like she was going to claw her eyes out. Charlotte just stood, arms crossed, tapping her toe like she was waiting on a train or for a commercial to be over.

"What are you raving about now?"

"You know dang well what I'm raving about."

Leonard closed the door, shaking his head. "What's going on?"

Catherine practically lunged at him. "I'll tell you what's going on. You need to get your wife on a leash over here."

"Excuse me?" Charlotte gasped.

"You heard me. You're out of control."

"What happened this time?" Leonard eyed Charlotte suspiciously. Charlotte just shrugged.

"Your idiot of a wife left parakeet seed stacked by my door so Cassie would realize I still have Marilyn. After we already agreed to keep it a secret. You know, that was the stupidest move ever because you have just as much to lose as I do."

"First of all, you have no proof I did anything of the sort."

"Like I need proof. We all know your vindictive ways."

"*My* vindictive ways? You're the one who stormed into my book club, calling my daughter names and gloating about her breakup with Joe. And then you proceeded to get my book club canceled. If anyone is a vindictive psycho, it's clearly you." Charlotte was screaming now. She wanted desperately to snap the finger Catherine had pointed in her face. She thought about it seriously, but decided Leonard might not approve.

"Well, it's on now. *Game on.* You better kiss your little flea bag good-bye."

"What, are you going to tell Cassie? I'm sure you already did. It won't work. I've got plans."

"I'm sure you do. But no, I didn't tell her. You'll be happy to know she didn't even question me about Marilyn. I just told her the birdseed was for the outdoor birds, and she bought it because she knows I'm trustworthy."

"Well, we never said Cassie was smart," Charlotte retorted, rolling her eyes.

"And don't think I was protecting you by not telling her. I just have better ideas. I'd rather strike at you when you're not expecting it."

"Sure you would. But it won't work. Do you know why? Because while you're too busy ordering expensive bags and couture shoes, I'll be using my intelligence to get ahead. You might be the so-called beauty of this place, but I'm the brains. You won't win."

"Brains? Are you kidding? Your family doesn't know

anything about brains. Look at your fool of a daughter, screwing up her relationship with my darling son. What an idiot."

"Sorry to break it to you, but things are working out. He's back home."

"Not for long, if I have any say. I'm going to talk some sense into that boy of mine. He can do so much better than that river rat of a daughter you have."

"You wretched crone!" Charlotte yelled, inching closer to Catherine, her face tightening with rage.

"Come on over, honey. This beauty packs a mean punch. Want to find out?" Catherine was ready for the offensive, heading toward Charlotte, who dodged out of the way.

"Ladies! That's enough. Now *damn it, sit the hell down!*" Leonard was shaking with anger, something so uncharacteristic for the amicable man. The two women actually froze, their fight temporarily taking a backseat to Leonard's outburst. They silently sat down at the kitchen table, gazes now glued to Leonard.

He exhaled. "It's about time you two listen to reason."

"Did you swear?" Catherine asked. "Because I think that's the first time I've ever heard you swear."

"What, now you're an expert on my husband?"

"Stop it," Leonard demanded. They zipped their lips. Leonard headed to the table, taking a seat between them.

"Now, we're going to have a civil conversation. And by civil conversation, I mean I'm going to talk at you and you are both going to be silent. Got it?"

No one said anything.

"Good. Now look. I've sat by and watched you two go at each other's throats. The competitions, the schemes, the angry words. I've patiently waited for this thing to work itself out. But you're family now, like it or not. You two need to stop being so damn selfish. You need to start minding your own business. Annie and Joe are adults. They can figure out their relationship on their own. They do not need you two dueling it out behind the scenes, and they don't need the stress you're both putting on them with this never-ending war. So get your acts together. If you can't be civil, then just ignore each other. I'm not going to sit by and watch you two self-destruct."

Catherine and Charlotte glared at each other. A long minute passed by, nothing but their breathing filling the silence.

"He's got a point," Charlotte almost growled through gritted teeth.

Catherine crossed her arms, nose in the air. "You always say that. How many times have we agreed to disagree? Never lasts. Sorry, Leonard. We'll try, but you know she's going to screw it up."

"I'm going to screw it up? Really?" Charlotte slammed a hand on the table. Horace meowed, startled.

"Charlotte," Leonard warned.

"Fine. Whatever. I won't start anything."

"Fine. I'm too busy to bother with peasants like you anyway," Catherine responded, grimacing at Charlotte. "I'm done here. I'm off to my fashion club meeting.

It's our first group meeting today, since the community room schedule is a little emptier with the loss of certain activities."

Catherine winked at Charlotte, who reminded herself to take some deep yoga breaths. Catherine dramatically clicked her heels on the linoleum the whole way to the apartment door, which she then shut a little too harshly.

Leonard and Charlotte stared at each other for a long moment before Charlotte did the only thing she knew to do in an aggravating situation like this.

She headed to the cupboard, grabbed the box of scones, and set them on the table. Leonard managed to grin as Charlotte helped herself to two before going back to the baby clothes.

Chapter Twenty-One

Amelia

Amelia traipsed through the apartment door. She had squeezed in a walk with Holly, but now it was time to get ready for her date with Owen. He would be home from work in a few hours.

He'd returned to his work at Wildflower Meadows, claiming he couldn't picture himself working anywhere else. The pay was only mediocre, but combined with Amelia's wages and money from songwriting, they'd be okay for a little while at least.

"Hey, how are you?" Janie greeted her at the door, a bag of chips in her hand. She was extra bubbly today. Not that she wasn't always exuberant.

"Okay. How are you?"

"I'm great. Awesome actually. I have super exciting news." The smile on Janie's face was contagious. Amelia felt it spread to her own face.

"What is it?"

"I met someone today. I have a date tomorrow night with him. Isn't that great?" Janie was jumping up and down, grabbing Amelia's hands. Amelia squealed.

"Details, please. What's he look like?"

"Gorgeous. Next question."

"How'd you meet?"

"He's a nursing intern. It was… I don't know, Amelia. We just hit it off, you know?"

Amelia smiled. "Oh, I know. Between those syringes and hospital gowns, wow, the sparks fly, huh?"

Janie groaned. "Oh, stop. It wasn't like that."

"Really?" Amelia raised an eyebrow.

"Well, okay. So I did have a syringe in my hand. But it didn't matter. I saw him, and I was just drawn to him. Does that sound cheesy?"

Amelia shook her head. "No, not at all. I'm excited for you. I hope it all works out. What's his name?"

"Eric."

Amelia eyed Janie with contentment. She recognized the sparkle in her eye, the glow in her cheeks. She'd felt that not long ago, too—the excitement of realizing she'd met someone special.

"This is great. I can't wait to hear the details after your date tomorrow." Amelia meant it. Despite her melancholy mood over the complexities her family was facing, she was thrilled at the prospect of Owen's sister finding a piece of her own happiness. She had come to love the girl as her own family. They'd forged a bond over Owen but had found a friendship because of the similarities between them.

"Yeah. It's exciting. I haven't had the best of luck with guys, so I don't want to get ahead of myself. But listen, I wanted to mention something else, too. I've started looking for apartments. I appreciate you guys letting me stay here, but I've been in town a while now. It's time I started finding my own groove, making my own life here. I'll be out of your hair soon enough. I know this living arrangement has been less than ideal for you guys."

"Janie, shut up. You don't have to leave on our account. We love having you here."

Janie arched an eyebrow. "Are you sure about that? Because last night, I'm pretty sure my brother was giving me the 'Don't you have somewhere to be' look after the movie."

"Well, yes, it can be a bit awkward with the space not being so big. But we manage. And I love having someone to share in my Pop-Tart and soap opera obsession."

"I love living here too. Trust me, I'm appreciative. But I'm gonna look for a new place soon. Once that little one comes, I think four might be a crowd in here."

Amelia grinned, her hand falling to her stomach, still pretty undetectable. "Well, I'm sure the couch is getting old too."

Janie scrunched her nose. "Um, yeah, it's not quite a luxury bed. But like I said, I'm appreciative. You're the best. I'm so glad you're in our family." Janie reached over to hug Amelia, and Amelia smiled again. She liked the thought of Janie being family.

"Okay, enough mushy stuff. Get to your room. Owen instructed me to leave the surprise in there."

"Surprise?" Amelia inquired.

"For your date. You two lovebirds have big plans for tonight."

"It's just a date."

"That's not what Owen said. He wants tonight to be perfect."

Amelia's heart sank a little with nerves. She'd heard this sentiment before when….

"Oh my God, Janie, he's not…."

Janie shook her head. "No, I don't think so. Owen's a terrible secret keeper, so I think I'd know. No, he just wants tonight to be perfect. He knows you've been stressing. He wants you guys to have fun tonight."

Amelia nodded. "Sounds wonderful. I miss spending time together."

"Well, then get your scrawny butt to your room and look at your surprise. Owen will be home soon, and if you aren't ready, he's going to blame me."

Amelia scampered back to their room, vowing to forget about all the complications with her mother and Joe. Tonight was about spending time with Owen, the father of her baby.

The man she had fallen in love with by the appetizers at an elderly woman's birthday party.

***

"Hot mama!" Janie proclaimed, wolf whistling when Amelia emerged twenty minutes later dressed in the outfit Owen had left for her.

The black dress clung to her body in all the right places, draping graciously over her stomach to hide any potential puffiness from her current state. The asymmetrical hem made her feel trendy, but the lacy straps accented the backless, sexy qualities of the dress. It was simple, it was in Amelia's favorite color. It was her.

"You're getting some tonight." Janie winked, eying up Amelia and making her feel self-conscious.

"Ew. He's your brother."

"Well, I didn't say I was getting some. So what's the problem? I'm not an idiot. I know what tonight's about." She winked again. Amelia couldn't help but chuckle.

"You're incorrigible."

"What's with you and that word? My brother's right. You are a word nerd."

Amelia headed over, playfully shoving Janie's shoulder. "So where's he taking me?"

"You'll have to ask him."

"I thought he wasn't good at keeping secrets. Didn't he tell you?"

"He's not and he did."

"So?" Amelia asked pointedly.

"So… my brother's not good at keeping secrets. But I am."

She headed back to her seat on her couch slash bed, turning on the television to *Days of Our Lives.*

Amelia didn't have long to wait to be whisked away to a night of romance. Two minutes later, a bouquet of red roses in hand, Owen sauntered through the door, letting out his own wolf whistle at the sight of her.

Janie broke the seriousness of the moment with a chuckle and an "I told you so."

Amelia smiled as Owen asked what they were talking about.

***

Amelia had been expecting a fancy dinner somewhere close, something simple to celebrate a night out.

But Owen had other plans.

"Tonight's about us having some fun, about us being spontaneous. Because yes, we didn't plan on settling in to this life we're about to settle into. But I want you to realize that just because we have a new title of parents, just because we're not traveling the world, doesn't mean we have to turn into these boring, washed-up adults. We're still us, Amelia. We're still the couple I love the most," he'd said as they were driving, radio blaring as usual.

Three hours of driving later, and Owen had slapped a blindfold on Amelia.

"Why?"

"Because I want you to be surprised. It's fun."

So she had complied, wearing the blindfold for the past fifteen minutes, hoping she didn't get nauseous from

Owen's erratic driving made all the worse by her not being able to see.

She trusted him, though.

The car stopped, and she felt Owen shift to park. "We're here."

"Can I take this off now?"

"Not yet. Hang tight."

Amelia let out a sigh, butterflies sinking in. A minute later, Owen was opening her car door. He reached for her hand, guiding her carefully out of the car. They walked, Amelia letting him guide her along. She tried to gauge where they were.

"A little further. Just a few more steps. Careful, careful," Owen goaded her with his voice as he pulled her toward him with his hands. The blindfold was itchy and she wanted to complain, but the excitement of the surprise kept her from whining.

"Okay, here we are."

There were loud noises and what sounded like children all around. She heard a bugle playing a punchy tune. There was a cacophony of laughter and announcements. She thought she heard someone say something about a kingdom and peasants.

"Where the hell are we?"

"Well, take off your blindfold and see."

At the command, Amelia ripped of the blindfold, anxious to see where the slinky black dress would fit in.

Her eyes took a few minutes to adjust to the sights around her. She was standing near what appeared to be a castle, a line of kids and adults gathered. Children shrieked as they played with pretend swords, and several regally dressed people manned the ticket booth. Her gaze moved upward, landing on the sign.

Medieval Times.

"Oh my God, really? You remembered?" She jumped up and down, giving the younger children in line a run for their money in the excitement department. A few calm adults eyed her suspiciously.

Owen grinned. "Yeah. I remember you saying you'd always wanted to go."

"Since junior high! I got sick the day of the field trip here. And then I just always felt like it was weird for a twentysomething to go here alone."

"Well, now you're a thirtysomething here, but you're not alone. And you're pregnant. So it's all okay."

She laughed, still jumping up and down. "Do we have good seats?"

"Front row, of course." He reached into his pocket, fanning the tickets.

She wrapped her arms around his neck. "This is awesome."

"Not too cheesy? I was worried it might not be romantic enough."

At that, she planted a passionate kiss on his lips, pulling back only when she remembered their venue. "It's perfect. I can't wait. It's going to be so much fun."

And she meant it. It felt good to do something a little strange, a little childish. This was why she'd fallen in love with Owen. He remembered things, details about her. And he wasn't afraid to have fun, to do something a little unconventional.

***

Three hours later, Amelia dashed after Owen as he pulled on her hand, leading her from the castle to the car. She laughed as she hobbled along in her ballet flats, yanking her dress up slightly to give her better movement. It had started to drizzle, but she didn't care. Now sporting one of the plastic crowns her younger counterparts in line had been wearing, she was feeling sheer elation.

"That was a blast," she yelled at Owen, childlike exuberance flooding her voice.

He looked back, smiling, as he led her carefully through the busy parking lot. The sun had set and the air had chilled, but they were both warm from the excitement of the show.

"Everything you hoped for?"

"And more. God, I'm stuffed though."

As they reached Owen's silver Chrysler, he opened the door for her.

"Well, you're eating for two, so you're allowed to indulge."

At the words, she didn't freeze up, didn't feel the familiar panic rising in her chest like it had recently. The evening with Owen, an evening of jousting and falcons, of pretend swordfights and roasted chicken, had soothed her. Sitting beside him as the dinner and tournament commenced, she saw a life with Owen not unfamiliar from the life she had once dreamed of. She saw a life of joy and laughter. Now there would just be an extra hand in hers, an extra seat at Medieval Times.

And if the child grew up to be anything like Owen, she knew it would be okay. They would be a family. A happy, fun-loving, medieval-tournament-attending family.

Once Owen got in the car, he turned on the headlights and the wiper blades.

"It's too bad our knight didn't win. I was hoping to get the rose," Amelia absentmindedly stated as she buckled her seat belt.

Owen glanced at her. "Oh, I think your need for roses will soon be quenched."

She eyed him curiously. "Really?"

"Yeah. At our next stop."

"Next stop? You mean home?"

"Come on, give me more credit than this. Medieval Times was a blast, but I told you we were having a romantic night. The night's not over yet."

"Really?" A grin flooded her face. She had thought their night *was* over. She was surprised by Owen's sense of romance.

"Really."

"So where are we headed?" she asked as he put the car in drive and pulled out, hitting the highway.

"You'll see."

Amelia gently shook her head, partially because she couldn't believe Owen had done all this for her, and partially because she couldn't believe she had doubted it would all work out. She was lucky. Her baby was lucky.

Everything was going to be more than fine. Despite the drizzle and the darkness, Amelia peered out the window and saw a vast life of bliss set before her.

***

"I can't believe you have me blindfolded again," she proclaimed twenty minutes later as she was led somewhere in secret. The elevator ride in her blindfold had been somewhat nauseating. Now, she felt uneasy. Owen led her. She felt safe holding on to his arm.

"Just a few more steps." He let go of her for one second to unlock a door and then led her forward. Stepping behind her, he gently kissed her neck as he unhooked the blindfold, revealing the second half of their evening.

They stood in a suite fancier than Amelia had ever seen. It was the type of hotel suite one saw in movies but never in real life. Now, there she stood, Owen's grin palpable as he leaned into her neck. Rose petals cascaded from the bed onto the floor, a gorgeous trail beckoning her forward. Candles illuminated the room in a soft glow, and two bouquets of roses adorned the nightstands. It was the scene every woman dreamed of but few actually experienced. It was a fairy tale, one Amelia had never dreamed would belong in her reality.

She turned to him, surprise on her face. "I can't believe you did all this," she whispered, wrapping her arms around his neck as she leaned in, nose to nose.

"I wanted to do something special. I know things have been rough lately, I know we've been sorting a lot out.

But Amelia, I love you. Always. Forever. And yes, life has already thrown us a few curveballs. But they're curveballs I'm happy about. Everything that happens to us is a gift because I'm going through it with you. I love you, I love our life. I love us. And I already love our baby."

He softly moved a hand to her stomach like he had done so many times before. But this time, it was different. This time, she could sense the glowing love he had for not only her, but for the life inside of her as well. He was right. This baby was a curveball. It was something she hadn't been expecting, something that terrified her. It was something she thought would tear them apart.

Standing in this romantic whirlwind with the man she had fallen hard for, she realized this baby was nothing of the sort. This baby was the sealing connection between Owen and her, a symbol for the world of their love. It was a symbol of their unwavering connection, of their undying passion for each other.

This baby changed everything, but it also kept everything the same.

"I love you," she whispered into his lips, the prickly stubble from his rugged beard scraping against her as she took his mouth with hers.

He kissed her back, passionately at first, feverishly next. He led her backward into the room, toward the bed dripping in rose petals. As he gently laid her over the duvet, climbing atop her, he looked deep into her eyes.

"I love you too." And then she succumbed to her

feelings and passions, her only thoughts Owen and the warmth flooding her soul as he claimed her one more time.

Chapter Twenty-Two

Amelia

Amelia awoke to the feel of unfamiliar sheets. She ran her hand over the satiny silk of the pillowcase, a far cry from the scratchy, bargain store cotton pillowcases adorning her own bed. As her eyes fluttered open, recollections of where she was and the night before oozed into her heavy mind. She smiled, turning over to face Owen, but the bed was empty.

Body sluggish from a night of passion, she remained quiet, breathing in the scent of his cologne left on the pillowcase.

Owen.

He had given her a night to remind her of what they had. He had gone through so much trouble to show her what she had already known.

Their love, their romance, wasn't going anywhere.

It was funny how one night could change everything, could remind you of what you had. She felt guilty he had spent so much, had gone through so much trouble, to give her a night of her romantic dreams. But then again, she'd needed it. She'd needed a night with him, a night to reconnect, to rediscover how good they were together, both emotionally and physically.

Not that they didn't or couldn't remember that at home in their simple apartment. Janie's presence had put somewhat of a damper on their love life. She was gone frequently, but the close quarters still made it awkward.

So it had been a great gift to spend the night reveling in each other, talking about the past and future, connecting with each other again. Alone in the fancy hotel suite, they had time to solely focus on each other, their love, and the connection that hadn't faded.

Groggily sitting up in bed, she leaned against the pillows and the classy headboard. She took inventory of the suite, looking for the man who had made all this possible.

Rustling her hands in her hair and covering herself with the comforter, she leaned forward to glance out the sliding glass doors. The curtains had been cracked open. She could see glimpses of Owen on their balcony, sitting on an outdoor chair, his phone in his hand. She smiled, thinking she should get some clothes on and join him, take in the view of the town from the balcony.

She saw him dial, though, and put the phone to his ear. She decided to lean her head back against the headboard, wait for him to finish his phone call. Maybe he could be persuaded to come back to bed just for a little while before they had to be heading home.

She heard him say, "Hey, Pete," and realized he was talking to his bandmate—or former bandmate, she corrected herself. Owen's voice was muffled, the glass door masking the intonation and enunciation of his words. But she could still eavesdrop with little effort.

Not that she was trying to. She was simply relaxing in the silence of the room, Owen's distant voice, sounding waterlogged, beckoning her to listen.

She heard them exchange some niceties and basics.

But then the conversation shifted. Pete must have asked Owen to come back to the band, must have been talking about the baby and the situation.

Because after a few more basic statements and some tiptoeing around, Owen said it. He said the truth to Pete he hadn't told Amelia, the truth Amelia had been fearing.

"Yeah, man, I know. It does suck. I'm devastated by it, to tell you the truth. This was my dream, you know? I hate that I had to walk away from it. But this is the right thing for us all. This baby changes everything. And as hard as it is, I can't be the selfish prick who puts himself first. I can't let my dream get in the way of my responsibilities. So this is just how it has to be."

Just as Amelia had feared, Owen wasn't feeling the fatherly need to raise this baby. He wasn't feeling a rush of heartwarming sentiment. He was feeling obligated, a sense of responsibility.

And he was devastated.

Tears formed in her eyes as she realized the truth, a truth she had almost let a few rose petals and some hot sex obliterate.

She was ruining Owen's life. She was ruining his dreams.

Well, she couldn't do it anymore. Owen might feel like he couldn't walk away.

But she knew what she had to do, now more than ever.

***

When Owen walked back in the room a few minutes later, Amelia was in the shower, lathering her hair and washing away both the previous night and the hopes she'd had. As the water swirled down the drain, she felt like all her lofty hopes went right along with it.

After toweling off, she put her dress from the night before back on. She hadn't brought anything else, and Owen hadn't thought ahead to bring her a change of clothes. She would be doing the walk of shame, but she didn't care. None of it mattered.

Tousling her hair as she scrunched it dry with the towel, she heard Owen approach her.

He snuck up behind her, wrapping his arms around her, leaning in for a kiss.

"Hey, baby. Morning," he said as he continued to kiss her neck.

She tried to feel nothing.

"Morning." She shrugged him off, heading to the room to get her things together.

Owen stood for a second, paused, her coldness probably throwing him off.

"Hey, everything okay? You seem distant."

"I'm fine. We should be going, right?" She didn't want to give it all away. She didn't want to talk to him now, didn't want to get into it. She tried to hold it together, her composure threatening to burst. She wouldn't do this here, wouldn't tarnish this memory for them. Plus, she wasn't prepared to spend several hours in the car in snotty, heart-wrenching tears.

This could wait a few more hours. This could wait until they were in the safety and security of what was once their home. She would wait.

As they gathered their things, Owen still looking puzzled, he pulled her in to him again. "Hey, look at me," he said. She obeyed. "I love you."

She looked up into his eyes, his gaze causing her chest to tighten. "I love you too, Owen," she replied honestly.

When she looked into his eyes, she did, in fact, see love. She saw herself, saw their life together.

Which made all this so much harder.

***

The ride home was tense, silent. Owen seemed to notice something was off but didn't say anything. He probably just attributed it to pregnancy hormones.

The car glided down the highway, soft rock music playing on the radio as she stared out the window. Unlike the night before, the skies had cleared and the drizzly gray weather had turned into a gorgeous, bright sky. But inside, Amelia felt like the weather from the night before was still ruling.

They pulled into the parking lot a few hours later, and as soon as she could, Amelia leaped out. Owen followed as she plodded up the steps to their apartment, tears threatening to flow. She opened the door, glad to see Janie wasn't inside. She wanted to be alone with Owen, to confront him without an audience.

He came in the door behind her, putting his keys on the counter before walking toward her. She stood in the middle of the living room.

"Amelia, hey. Talk to me. You've been quiet since this morning. What's wrong?" He walked toward her, ready to put his arms around her, concern on his face.

She took a step back that said everything.

Tears welled in her eyes. She stood her ground. "I heard you this morning."

Confusion sweeping over his face, he looked at her, silent, thinking. Then confusion shifted to recognition, his eyes brightening with clarity. "What did you hear?"

Tears now rolled down her face. She'd been strong, held it in for the ride home. Now, surrounded by their familiar things, surrounded by the promises of a life that was supposed to be forever theirs, her stoic façade faded.

"Everything. I heard everything. And I can't do this anymore."

He walked toward her. "Amelia, listen. It's not what it

sounded like. Pete was just giving me a hard time. I just needed him to know I was done. That's all. I didn't want him thinking I was coming back."

Amelia nodded, not even angry. She didn't blame him for this. "Owen, I heard you. You said you were devastated, that this sucked. The thing is, I heard you before you even said it. I heard it before I even told you I was pregnant. I know you, Owen. I know what you want in life. I know how the band is everything to you. That's part of the reason I fell in love with you... your drive, your passion for your music. This is why I didn't even want to tell you about the baby. I knew it would ruin everything for you. And I also knew you were too good of a guy to do anything but let this ruin your career."

Owen vehemently shook his head. "You've got it wrong, Amelia. It's not what it sounded like. Of course I'm sad about leaving the band. But I'm thrilled with this, with us. I want this."

"But if you could choose, you'd still be in the band."

He eyed her, proceeding cautiously. "I loved the band, Amelia. You know that. But I love you and this baby more."

"I'm not going to be the one to rip you from this dream."

"It's not your choice."

"I'm making it my choice. Owen, we're done. I'm leaving. I can't be the reason you quit. I can't be the reason you're devastated. I can't make you stay out of a sense of responsibility. I love you. And I know you love me. But I won't be the reason your dream is over. Go back to the band. I'll raise the baby."

"Amelia, you're acting crazy. Stop it."

He walked toward her again, but she shoved him. "Go, Owen. Go back to the band."

"That's not what I want."

"Well, it's what I want. I don't want you here."

"You don't mean it, Amelia. Look, I'm sorry for what I said. I shouldn't have worded it like that."

"No, you *should* have. Because it's what you meant."

"No, it's not."

"Owen, leave. Go."

"I won't. Stop it. I love you."

"I know. But this isn't going to work. Now leave, or I will."

"I'm not leaving."

She paused, taking a long glance at him. "Then I'm leaving."

"Don't do this."

"It's for you."

Before he could stop her, Amelia pushed past him, grabbing her bag and headed down the stairs to her car. He tried to follow, but she slammed the door in his face. She heard it swing open as she descended the stairs, but her sobs prevented her from hearing exactly what he yelled after her. She passed Janie on the way out of the building.

"Amelia?" she asked, confusion and panic flooding the girl's face.

Amelia stopped for a second to look at Janie, the girl who had become her friend. "It's over." That was all she could muster. Janie eyed her curiously, her brow furrowed, before Amelia headed to her car, started the engine, and drove away.

Chapter Twenty-Three

Annie

With her leggings and an oversized T-shirt on, Annie slowly peeled herself from the sofa and her soap operas to answer the door. She wasn't sure who would be visiting her at this time on a Saturday afternoon, but whoever it was, they were insistent; the doorbell had rung three times in a row.

"I'm coming," she shouted as Peter and Butternut ran crying to the door. They were worse than dogs when it came to company.

When she threw back the door, self-consciously readjusting her shirt and trying not to worry about her shoddy appearance, she froze. It was Amelia.

And she looked terrible.

Mascara streaked down the girl's face. She had on a gorgeous, skintight black dress—but it looked like she'd slept in it. Her hair had the messy, hasn't-been-washed-in-a-few-days look.

But her face. The pale face, the bloodshot eyes. This was clearly a girl who needed her mother.

"Amelia, what is it? What's wrong? Is it the baby? Is everything okay?" Panic usurped all of Annie's ability to reason. Her gaze pierced into Amelia, trying to decipher the issue.

Amelia just shook her head, slowly entering, sniffling as she brushed right by the meowing Butternut and Peter. Amelia led herself to the couch and plopped herself down. Looked like Annie wasn't the only one having trouble in paradise.

"Is Joe here? I'm sorry if I'm interrupting," Amelia croaked out, her voice sounding crinkly.

"No, he went fishing for the afternoon."

Amelia stared blankly ahead. "So are things better?"

"Not really. Things are still a wreck. But we're moving in the right direction. He's at least back in the house. But we're not talking about me. What's going on with you? What's wrong?"

Amelia just continued to stare as Annie sat on the couch beside her daughter, taking her in her arms.

"It's over, Mom. We're over."

"What are you talking about? What happened?"

Amelia shrugged. "I can't do it anymore. I can't take

his dreams from him."

"Amelia, you're being ridiculous. You know—"

Amelia cut her off. "Mom, stop. Everyone keeps trying to tell me he loves me, and that I'm crazy. I know he loves me. I do. But I can't make him give up everything for me, for this life. This isn't what he wants. And I won't be married to a man who has regrets because of me."

Annie paused, thinking. She knew a thing or two about regrets. She knew a thing or two about being married to a man who wanted something else. So she understood. She got it, got where Amelia was coming from.

She didn't argue, didn't say a word. She just took Amelia in her arms and hugged her.

"You can stay for as long as you want."

Tears flowed down Amelia's cheeks as she sobbed into her mom's shirt. "I love him. I hate this."

"Listen. Just take some time to sort through it all. Take some time away from everything. Stay with us for a bit. It'll be okay. No matter what, you're going to be okay. You'll figure it out."

Amelia pulled back to look at her mother. "We've sure screwed things up, huh?"

Annie smiled. "Yeah, we did. But I think I screwed up worse than you."

Annie sat for a few minutes, staring blankly, thinking about how messy both their lives had gotten. They'd both found love in unexpected places only to be sitting here now, confused and feeling alone.

"Love is overrated, huh?" Amelia said finally,

breaking the silence.

Annie sighed. "Sometimes, yes."

Amelia wiped the tears from her eyes, her sobs calming now to neutrality. "Have you seen Dad?"

"Amelia, we don't need to talk about this now."

"Why not? You're sure okay with talking about me and why I'm upset. And here you are, not in much better shape."

"What's that supposed to mean?"

"Mom, look at what you're wearing. On a Saturday. Alone."

"That's kind of the state of things lately. Alone."

"So answer me. Have you seen Dad?"

"No. I cut things off."

"Good."

Annie sighed, staring blankly ahead. "Amelia, it wasn't what you think. I was just trying to help him."

"By making out with him?"

"It wasn't like that."

"That's not what Grandma Charlotte told me."

"And do you always listen to Grandma Charlotte?"

"She usually knows what she's talking about."

Annie grimaced. "Yeah, you're right. She was certainly right about me and Dave being a bad idea."

"Well anyone could've told you that. Doesn't take a rocket scientist. What were you thinking?"

"I wasn't. Well, that's not true. I was thinking I could help him. I was thinking I owed him that much."

Amelia laughed out loud. "Owed him? After he

screwed you over? You're an idiot, Mom."

"You're right. I was an idiot. And now I almost lost the best thing that's ever happened to me. I still could. Maybe that's what your dad wanted. Maybe he didn't want to see me happy."

"You're not going to lose Joe. He's back, isn't he? That's a step."

"He's back. But not emotionally. He doesn't trust me. And I can't blame him. We sit around, the silence deafening me. He can't even look at me."

"Give it time."

"It's been weeks."

"He's probably just worried you're going to go back to Dad. You just need to show him you're committed."

"How am I supposed to do that when he won't look at me, won't touch me? He's sleeping in the guest room."

"Okay, Mom, I didn't need to know that. Keep your intimate details to yourself."

"I don't want to hear it about keeping intimacy to yourself. My eyes are still burning from last year when I walked in on that fiery kiss."

Amelia closed her eyes, shaking her head. "Can we not?"

"You're right. I'm done, I'm done." The two smiled, eventually turning to full-fledged laughter.

"Our lives *are* a mess, huh?" Annie said, leaning in to Amelia.

"Yep. But what else would we expect?"

"At least Grandma's love life is doing well."

"Is that supposed to make me feel better? That an eightysomething is having a better love life than me right now?"

"It is pretty sad, huh?" Annie stood up now, heading to the kitchen.

"Where are you going?"

"To get some popcorn."

"Popcorn?"

"Yes. I'm tired of the tears and the sad talks about love. We need some laughs."

"What are you proposing?"

Annie turned on her way to the kitchen, eying her daughter. She gave her a look that questioned her sanity. A look of recognition flooded Amelia's face.

They both grinned, tears now gone.

"*Bridesmaids*!" they both said at the same time, bursting into adolescent giggles.

Chapter Twenty-Four

Annie

Tears streamed down Annie's and Amelia's face, but they were of a different variety than a few hours ago. Gone were the worries and what-ifs about Owen and Joe. Amelia seemed to have forgotten about the dream killing she was worried about, her face lit up with a toothy grin at her favorite scene, the giant cookie scene. Annie also laughed loudly at the ridiculous antics on screen. This was just what they needed.

Cuddled up under her favorite red throw with her daughter, Annie let go of some of the tension she'd been holding in. Things with Joe were bad, sure. But it could be worse. At least she still had her daughter, her family.

Amelia was right. Joe would come around.

Annie still felt guilty about what had happened. She hated what she'd done to him, to their new marriage. She'd done the exact thing Dave had done to her—okay, so she hadn't slept around, but she'd betrayed Joe's trust. It was the same thing. Annie hated what had become of their simple, carefree love. She hated that in a way, Dave had ruined her love life twice now.

But she knew it wasn't all Dave's fault.

She'd made the decision to open the front door when Dave first came. She'd made the decision to let him in every time after that. She'd made the decision to lie to Joe about it. Most importantly, she'd made the decision to lock lips with Dave.

Despite the chaos it had caused, though, she was, in an odd way, thankful for the kiss. It had done a few things for her. First, it had shown her that yes, there would always be feelings between her and Dave. It was ridiculous to think there wouldn't be. He'd been her husband for so many years. How could the passion just die because of a crazy, messy situation?

It couldn't.

He'd put her through hell, had betrayed her in every way. But no matter what, that couldn't negate their life together. It didn't take away all the memories, moments, and feelings that had kept them together so long. It didn't obliterate him from her past, from every moment of her adult years. Even if she wanted his mistake to destroy all attachments she had to him, it simply couldn't. That was something she would have to live with.

Second, and more importantly, the kiss had reminded her of what she had with Joe.

Because during that kiss, during those awful moments afterward, a serious revelation had slammed into her. Yes, she would always have feelings for Dave, would always feel something for him.

But he would never be Joe.

The way her lips felt on Dave's was nothing in comparison to the way they felt on Joe's. With Dave, she felt a fleeting passion from something that had once been. With Joe, though, she felt a safety and warmth hinting at the promised future.

She hated that it had taken a betrayal and a near breakup with Joe for her to realize this. But now that she had, she knew she would do anything to get them back on track. She'd cut Dave out of her life completely, refusing to even speak to him. He would have to maneuver the life of single parenthood alone. He'd made his decision.

And now she'd made hers. The past was the past. She was ready to look forward.

Now she just had to get Joe back on board, had to earn his heart back, had to help him find forgiveness for her.

As the final credits rolled and Amelia hummed along with the closing song, the door flew open, and Annie's future walked in.

***

"Hi, Joe," Amelia offered, rising from the couch to greet him. "How are you?"

He nodded at her, a genuine smile on his face. "Good. Caught a few fish today. What are you two doing?"

"Trying to forget how shitty my life is right now," Amelia said matter-of-factly.

Joe raised an eyebrow. "Popcorn and *Bridesmaids* can do that for you? I should give it a try."

Annie winced at the obvious dig.

Amelia eyed Joe as if she weren't sure what to do. She opened her mouth to say something only to stop. Finally, though, as Annie clicked off the television, Amelia spoke up.

"Listen, Joe. This is none of my business. But I've just had a terrible day with Owen and I'm feeling like crap about love, so I just have to get this off my chest. Forgive my mom. She was an idiot. She knows that. She doesn't love my dad. She loves you."

"Amelia," Annie interrupted, but Amelia hushed her.

"Now, I know you two are having a rough time, and I get it. I'd be pissed too, Joe. She screwed up big-time. But she loves you. She's miserable. You're miserable. Life's too short to be miserable. So please just forgive her and be happy again. I can't take any more relationships falling apart."

Joe eyed up Amelia before turning his gaze to Annie. After a tense pause, he spoke softly. "Is she right?"

Annie took a step forward, feeling like she were also taking a figurative step back toward Joe. "Yes. She's right, about everything. I was a fool. I let myself get caught up in running to Dave's aid. I let myself get swept up in a past I don't even want anymore. I love you. All of you. Dave's in the past. I want you to be my future again."

Joe stood, gazing at her. She could feel his defenses lifting. The wall that had crept between them was crumbling. He took a few steps toward her, and Amelia backed up to give them a moment.

He cautiously pulled her into his arms. "That kiss, seeing you two together, it killed me. I love you, Annie. I don't want to lose you. But I have to ask. Are you sure about us? Are you sure you don't want Dave now that he's available?"

Annie quickly shook her head. "Not a chance. He doesn't have my heart anymore. In all honesty, I don't think he ever did. I think it was waiting for you."

With that, Joe pulled her in for a kiss, a kiss probably more passionate than was appropriate with Amelia standing a few feet away. But Annie didn't care right now. She didn't care that her hair was a tad oily or that her T-shirt had some popcorn grease on it. She didn't care that they still had a lot to sort out, that it would probably be a long road to total and complete trust again.

All she cared about was that the man holding her was the man she wanted to be with, the man who meant everything to her. As he pulled away from her, she realized how lucky she was to have such a gentle soul in her life, a man who could forgive her worst transgressions, a man who could see her heart for what it was.

"I love you," she whispered through salty lips.

He just kissed her again.

"Okay, guys, seriously. Get a room," Amelia interrupted, and they pulled apart.

Before they could retort with an "Okay" and head upstairs, though, the doorbell rang.

"Who the hell is that?" Annie asked.

"I bet I have an idea," Amelia replied, panic on her face.

"I suppose I'll get it?" Joe asked, heading to the door.

"Joe, I'm not—" Amelia started, but before she could get out the final word, guitar music flooded the room.

"What the…?" Joe blurted, but Owen just strolled right past him, heading toward Amelia as if she were the only one in the room.

"Owen, what the hell are you doing?" Amelia asked, anger resonating in her voice.

Owen calmly, coolly kept strumming. "Getting you back."

"What are you talking about? Can you put the guitar down?"

"No."

Annie and Joe backed up behind the sofa, giving the two space but still staring. It was their turn to observe now.

"Why not? What are you doing?"

"Getting your attention."

"Why?"

"Because this seems to be the only way you'll listen."

"Owen, really? This is stupid."

Owen kept strumming, standing directly in front of her. He ignored her scowl, a confident grin taking his face. And then he started singing.

It wasn't just any song. It was the song that had tied them together, had united them as one entity moving toward a singular dream.

Amelia stopped, tears filling her eyes. Anger dissipated as she stared into Owen's eyes, listening to him sing. Annie also teared up, finally understanding what Owen was doing. She smiled as Joe put his arm around her.

When the song was over, Owen took off his guitar and got down on one knee.

"Owen, what the hell? *What* are you doing?" Tears were flowing down Amelia's face again.

"I know the timing is unconventional. I know we essentially just broke up because I was an idiot and said some really stupid things. So everything in me says this is the dumbest thing I could do right now, that no sane man would do this at this time."

Amelia nodded in agreement.

Owen continued. "So naturally, I'm going to do it now. Because that's how I roll. I don't do conventional, I don't do mainstream. I do what I want when I want to. So Amelia, when I say I want you, all of you, when I say I want this over the band, I mean it. Because I don't do anything for show or because it's what society says is right. You know that about me. That's what you claim to love about me."

Amelia nodded softly again, a stupefied look on her face.

"That song I just sang, it was a symbol of what we are together. Two people with crazy dreams who, individually, seem hopeless. But look what happens when we come together. We make music. We make magic. That's what I want for the rest of my life. I don't care if we do it in Amsterdam or if we do it on a tour bus or if we do it here with a white picket fence and apple pies in the oven. I want a life with you, with our baby, no matter what that looks like. Amelia, I know you're worried about my dreams. But listen, a few years ago, you'd have been right. My biggest dream was to be a singer in the band. That was it. And then I met you. Everything changed. Now, yeah, I still dream of singing. But without you, that dream doesn't mean anything. You're the dream now, Amelia. You're it. Everything else is secondary." He shifted his weight. "Sorry, I didn't expect to blabber on for so long." He grinned at her, looking back now to also grin at Joe and Annie. He shrugged. Annie smiled at him, tears filling her eyes.

Amelia just stared.

"Life is never easy or predictable. There are going to be so many changes. But I want to experience them all with you. I want to be ninety and still have you by my side, telling me how incorrigible I am. I want grandkids running around asking to see our tattoos and asking us to sing our song to them. I want it all. With you. Whatever that looks like. So stop worrying about me and my dreams. Stop worrying about being unconventional. Do something a little conventional for me, will you? Do something that will seal the deal for us, will prove we're in it for good, dreams or not." He pulled something from his pocket now. It wasn't the typical black box, Annie noticed. It was what appeared to be a handkerchief. But from the handkerchief, he pulled out a ring.

"Amelia, will you marry me? Make my wildest dreams come true?"

Amelia sobbed now, sinking down to the floor, eye to eye with him.

There was a long pause where Annie didn't quite know what to expect.

And then the word came out, the word everyone was waiting for.

"Yes."

Owen yelled his own, "Yes," sliding the ring on her finger. He kissed Amelia wildly, passionately, putting Annie and Joe's kiss to shame. Then, he helped Amelia up and picked her up, swinging her in a circle.

"Careful," Annie warned, the mother in her now stepping in.

"You're right, sorry," Owen abashedly smiled, putting Amelia down delicately and patting her stomach. He crept down on his knees, eye level with Amelia's stomach. "You hear that, Junior? Your mom's marrying me!"

Amelia laughed, ruffling his hair.

"Okay, enough, enough. Get over here!" Annie beckoned Amelia and Owen over, a smile widening on her face. She grabbed Amelia first, hugging her and congratulating her, only pulling back to see the ring. It was a gorgeous ruby ring circled by beautiful diamond chips.

"This is gorgeous, Owen."

"Thanks. It was my mom's."

Amelia's smile widened, but she looked worried now. "Owen, are you sure Janie doesn't want it? I love it, but I feel bad taking a family heirloom."

"Are you kidding? Janie was the one who gave it to me this afternoon. Her exact words were, 'If you don't head over there right now and put this ring on that girl's finger, I'm going to punch you until you bleed.'" Owen laughed.

"Well, I'm glad she knocked some sense into you," Amelia said, laughing.

"Sense into me? You're the one who broke up with me," he teased. There were no hard feelings, though. The two had fallen back into the familiar, friendly rut.

"Well, you're the one who proposed on the same day. I'm never letting our children forget this, you know. Such a romantic you are. Who proposes on the day of our first major fight?"

"Fight? You two were apart for what, like five hours? Some fight," Joe teased, now adding his two cents.

"Wait a second, did you say children?" Owen grinned.

"Child. I said child."

"You said children. I think you're getting used to this whole childrearing thing already. So what, you thinking like five? Six?"

"Bite your tongue. I haven't even been through labor yet. If it's anything like I've heard, I think you'll be lucky to get one out of me." Amelia turned away from Annie now, falling back into Owen's arms.

"Oh, I think I could change your mind," he muttered, his grin only widening.

"Now who needs to get a room?" Joe teased.

"Don't mind if we do," Owen replied, leading Amelia away.

"Honey?"

Amelia stopped, turning to face Annie.

"Yeah, Mom?"

"I'm glad things aren't so screwed up for us anymore." They both smiled at each other. "I'm so happy for you. Everything's working out."

"Yeah. It is. And I'm glad. Love you, Mom. I'll call you tomorrow."

"Okay. Oh, and Amelia?"

"Yes?"

"No giant cookies at your wedding shower, okay?"

"Don't count on it." They both laughed, Owen and Joe looking at each other and shrugging.

Amelia and Owen ran out the door, laughing in glee.

Annie sighed in happiness. It was amazing what a few hours could do to a relationship, for better or worse. She was just glad that today, it was for the better. For all of them.

"Looks like we can go get that room now?" Annie asked Joe. He pulled her up the stairs.

"I'm glad things worked out." Joe kissed her neck, slipping his hands under her T-shirt when they got to their room.

"Me too. It's good to see them so happy."

"I was talking about us." His hands moved to her back, unclasping her bra.

Annie smiled, wrapping her arms around his neck, leading him backward to the bed. "Yeah, it is. I've missed this."

"Oh yeah?"

"Yeah. It seems we've been missing out on our newlywed stage."

"Well, maybe we could make up for it?"

Joe stopped for a moment, looking deeply into Annie's eyes as she gazed back, still wrapped in his arms. "I love you, Annie. And I know this past year has been unexpected, in good and bad ways. I know you had a lot of history with Dave. I know it's not something you just forget. But I love you, and if we're going to make this work, it needs to be just us in this marriage."

"It is. I'm sorry, Joe. I really am… it's just—"

He cut off her sentence with a kiss before saying, "I know, Annie. I know. I love you."

They fell onto the bed together, succumbing to the roller coaster of the afternoon by getting on a completely different roller coaster of emotion.

Chapter Twenty-Five

Amelia
SEVEN MONTHS LATER

Amelia glanced in the mirror, her fingers running over her stomach as she stared. Despite her obedience to Annie's suggestion to use special lotions, she could see stretch marks. Her legs looked chunky, and her body was almost unrecognizable. She wanted to cry.

But then she ran her fingers over the bump and marveled at the kick she felt. There was a real, live human being in there. A human being she'd made with Owen. A human being she would raise with him, would love with him. It was miraculous.

She had always scoffed at the women who said a baby changed everything. How clichéd and utterly mushy.

How annoying, actually. She had a great life, or she had thought so before this turn of events. She didn't want to change everything.

And then the news. The initial shock, the confession. The morning sickness, the appointments.

The love.

It had snuck up on her, a creeping vine into her heart. Before she knew what had happened, her heart was completely overpowered by this tiny child she didn't even know. Nothing else before this point even seemed to matter anymore. It was all about the baby. Baby Charlotte had changed her whole world… and she wasn't even born.

There was an unfortunate accompaniment, though, to these euphoric, loving, motherly feelings.

Panic.

The terror, the utter fear that plagued Amelia the night she'd walked into her grandma's apartment late at night was all still there. It resonated within her when she heard other moms talking about colic and diaper rashes and other things so foreign to Amelia. It surged in her at the grocery store when a baby's screams tore right through her rationale and she wondered how anyone could handle a newborn. She worried when the questions flowed through her brain late at night—questions about bathing and bedtimes, choking hazards and preschools. There was so much to learn, so much to know. And the stakes were high.

For God's sake, she was going to be responsible for

someone else's life and well-being. She couldn't afford to screw up.

She'd read baby books. She'd talked to her mother. But as the day drew closer, she realized the gap of what she knew and what she needed to know only seemed to widen. How did anyone manage this?

Owen, of course, wasn't really worried. But wasn't that the stereotypical dad? *Worry about it later, we'll figure it out. It can't be that hard.* She'd seen the memes about dads and babies. But it was funny if a dad accidentally put a baby's shirt on backward or entertained her with a fake video game controller.

She was a woman and, thus, such behaviors would be deemed inexcusable. She was expected to know what she was doing. The whole mothering-instinct scenario. Amelia, though, couldn't help but wonder if it had skipped her. She didn't seem to have any mothering sense naturally within her.

There were other worries, too, about how things would change with Owen. She knew a baby changed everything—she'd seen enough diaper commercials to know this—but did it really have to change *everything?* She was still exploring this love with Owen. They were still finding themselves as a couple. Could they afford for everything to change already? Were they doomed because the stresses and changes would obliterate their relationship, which was already somewhat unsteady?

Owen snuck in behind her, and she saw his face in the mirror.

"What are you doing? You look so serious," he said, wrapping his arms around her midsection. She self-consciously pulled her shirt down and offered a weak smile, still looking at him in the mirror.

"I'm looking at how huge I am and wondering how long it's going to take on the treadmill to get back to a socially acceptable weight." He kissed her neck now, sending a shiver down her spine. She spun around in his arms, leaning into him.

"Stop it. You're beautiful."

"And you're a liar. Or a flirt."

"I prefer the second title."

He kissed her then, hard and passionately, leaning her against the sink counter. She fed into the kiss, savoring the passion between them. As they kissed, Amelia couldn't help but worry that in a few short weeks, these moments would be gone.

***

A few hours later, the couple stood in the center of the purple room that would soon be the nursery. Owen had painted it a few weeks ago—Amelia had slept at Annie's at the insistence of all family members. Now, it was time to put up the finishing touches.

Amelia fingered the tiny clothes, holding them to her nose to smell them as she folded them to put in the drawers. She smiled, knowing the next time she smelled them, they would have the smell of a newborn, a scent that stirred her—despite her self-proclaimed lack of maternal instincts.

Tucking the baby clothes carefully away, she picked up the teddy bear sitting on the rocking chair in the corner. Emotion swept over her as she fluffed its fur. It was just a simple bear, nothing special really to an outsider—but to Amelia, it was so much more. It was the symbol that everything in her life was, in fact, coming together.

The bear had been a gift from her father, a gift for baby Charlotte.

A while ago, she'd have never dreamed that bear would be sitting in her baby's nursery, never dreamed she'd be feeling emotional at the thought of her father being back in her life. She'd been angry, hurt. She'd felt split in half the moment she'd found out who her father truly was, and she'd had a hard time repairing herself. He'd hurt her mother, and he'd hurt her. It didn't matter that she was in her thirties. She felt like a teenager, ripped apart emotionally by an ugly divorce. The picture-perfect image of her parents, of love, of their family had been shredded by his senseless, hurtful acts. It was unforgivable.

Or so she had thought.

It had taken time, a lot of anger, and most importantly, Owen, to help her heal that rift, to help her realize she needed to forgive her father.

Slowly, she'd been bridging the gap between them, father and daughter. It was a painstaking process, one that had started with the appearance of her father at her door after the kiss. Amelia had sorted through many layers of grief, anger, and frustration. She'd faltered more than once, changed her mind. But, with the help of her maternal instincts kicking in, she'd started to realize the bond between a parent and child couldn't just go away. No matter what he'd done, no matter what choices he'd made, he was her dad, and she needed him. With Owen's help, she'd realized how precious a parent-child relationship could be.

Their formal healing had started over a cup of coffee a month back. She'd called him on a whim, nervous, feeling like she was being reunited with her father for the first time. In some ways, she was. They'd both changed so much over the past few years; they were practically strangers. Slowly, they'd been able to overcome the distance, to fight past old hurts, to rediscover each other. Things weren't perfect, like everything else in her life. They weren't attending father-daughter dances and she wasn't calling him every day of the week, but it was a start.

The teddy bear had been left by their door yesterday. They'd found it when they came home from shopping, along with a simple note.

For my granddaughter.

Love, Dad

It was crazy that five words and a stuffed animal could shift things in Amelia, could help her realize how right Owen was. She needed her dad, his horrible faults and all. She needed him in her life, not just for herself, but for her daughter. Her daughter deserved to know every piece of her family, to know where she came from.

Sitting the teddy bear back down, she turned from her thoughts, the wave of emotion shifting as she focused on Owen.

Owen hammered a nail in the wall, hanging a print of a silver guitar above the baby's crib. It had been a gift from the band. He stood back, assessing the levelness of his work, and Amelia turned to examine it, too.

"Looks great. I love that."

Owen turned around, hammer in his hand. "I love you."

She put the baby clothes down. "Can you believe she'll be here, in this room, any day now? It's absurd."

"I can't wait."

Amelia sighed. Her eyes averted to the floor.

"Hey," Owen said, walking toward her. "What's wrong?"

"I just feel like a jerk. Because you're so excited. And I am too. I really am. But more than that, I'm terrified."

"Hey, it's natural. You're allowed to be. After all, you're the one going through hours of labor, right?"

"Thanks for reminding me."

"I will allow you to squeeze my hand as hard as you want. So I mean, I think you're getting the better deal, right?"

"I hate you," Amelia said, punching him playfully but smiling. "But it's not even that. I'm terrified about the after labor part. About the parenting part. What if we don't know what we're doing?"

"I'm going to tell you a little secret. No one knows

what they're doing. And those people who post those lovely, cheesy pictures on social media of family game night and angelic sleeping babies… they're liars. End of story."

They interlaced fingers now, standing across from each other in the center of the soft, plush carpet, also freshly installed.

"I just want us to do a good job. I want her to have a good life. And I want us to have a good life."

"We will. I promise."

She nodded now, his simple words doing the trick. "You're right. It's just hormones."

He smiled, the few days' worth of stubble accenting his grin in an overtly sexy way. "Listen, while we're taking a little break, I want to give you something."

"What is it?"

"Wait here."

A few minutes later, Owen proudly strutted back into the room with an envelope.

"What is it?"

"Open it."

She peeled open the envelope to reveal a printout from the Hershey Hotel. Her face lit up as she read. "An all-inclusive, two-night stay at Hotel Hershey. Breakfast, lunch, and dinner included as well as the ultimate spa experience. A trip to the chocolate factory and Zoo America also included. Oh my God, Owen, you remembered!"

She'd mentioned a few months back how she'd

always wanted to stay at Hershey after her friends at Book World had talked about it being amazing. This was her dream getaway. He'd remembered. "When are we going?"

"This weekend. I think the stars call it a babymoon. I'm just calling it awesome. Chocolate, gourmet food, spa treatments, and an awesome suite with this sexy stud. What else could you want?"

"Nothing. Absolutely nothing."

She fell into his arms, her belly bumping against his firm abs. "I love you. I love our life," she said. Her worries dissipated in his arms. They would be more than fine. Everything was going to be perfect.

And even if it wasn't, she had Owen by her side. What more did she need?

Chapter Twenty-Six

Amelia

The scent of chocolate still lingered in Amelia's nose as she sank into the couples' bath in their private suite. They'd finished the chocolate facials and pedicures. They'd had a wonderful couples' massage and a gorgeous five-star dinner. Now, they were back in the room, alone, surrounded by beautiful linens and plush carpets. Amelia was, quite simply, floating. Chocolate bubble bath scented the air around them. It truly was a magical place.

Owen kissed her neck, the water splashing as he lifted a sudsy hand to move her hair softly to the side. She leaned back into him, the warmth of the water caressing her body. Suddenly, it didn't matter that she was feeling pudgy or hormonal or frightened. All she felt was relaxation, peace, and love.

"You're beautiful," Owen whispered into her hair, and she took a deep soothing, breath.

"This is beautiful. Thank you for doing this. This is exactly what I needed."

They sat, Owen embracing her in the warm water, for a few moments. She was the one to break the silence.

"Promise me we'll always be like this."

"What do you mean? Of course we will."

She turned to look up into his face, sinking down slightly to get more comfortable. "I'm serious, Owen. Promise me."

"Honey, why wouldn't we be? I'm crazy about you. I have been since the first day we met. I always will be."

"It's just, I'm worried. I'm worried because everyone says a baby changes everything. I don't want it to change us."

He touched her nose, a sparkle in his eye. "But it will change us. For the better. This baby will make us even stronger. Sure, it might be tougher to relax in a romantic tub like this every day. We might get tired and frustrated and stressed. But it's not going to change us at the core. Because no matter what, Amelia, I love you more than anything. I think you're gorgeous and smart. You complete me. This baby is going to add to our lives, not take away from it."

She smiled. "I hope you're right. Because I never

want to lose this."

"You won't." And then he kissed her with so much fervor, she couldn't dare dream things between them would ever change. He was right. There was a foundation of love between them. Nothing would change it.

When the water started to chill, they carefully got out, draining the tub, drying off, and wrapping in the lovely robes left for them. They climbed into the bed, Amelia yawning but not quite ready to let go of the night. She scarfed down the chocolate on her pillow as Owen did the same, peeling back the satiny sheets and climbing between.

She lay on her side, Owen holding her like he did so many nights. Usually, he had trouble keeping his hands off her, which she enjoyed. Tonight, though, there was a gentle sweetness between them. Neither seemed to want things to go further. They were content just being together, holding each other in the magic of the weekend away. They didn't need physicality to seal what they had. This weekend was about an emotional reconnection.

She stroked his arm with her free hand, lulling herself into a state of serenity.

"What do you think she'll be like?" she asked, one of her favorite questions of late. Owen was always willing to humor her, to play along.

"Well, I think she'll have to be gorgeous from the get-go. She'll take after her mom, after all."

"But I hope she has your eyes."

"I hope she has your nose."

"I hope she doesn't have your ears." Amelia giggled. This had become somewhat of a joke between them.

He poked her side lightly. "There is nothing wrong with my ears."

"Um, they are a little pointy."

"Elf ears are in, anyway," he said mockingly. "Seriously, though, Amelia. I hope she looks like you. But sometimes I don't. Because if she looks like you, when she grows up, I am going to have to carry a rifle around town to scare the boys away from her."

"You will do no such thing."

"You're right. Because you'll probably get to it before me."

"True. I can't imagine dating years. I don't want to think about it, remembering what I was like during that time. Oh, I hope karma doesn't come for me."

"Do you think she'll like pink?"

"Is it bad that I hope not?" Amelia asked, turning over to face him, stroking his face gently before resting her hands under her chin.

"It's just so crazy to me, to think about the fact this little human will be ours soon. We'll be there to see all her firsts, to learn about her, to see her personality develop."

"It is a scary, crazy beautiful thought, huh? I'm looking forward to so many moments."

"Amelia, we're going to have a blast. We are. The zoo, parades, first teeth, first time seeing Santa. I can't wait for every moment. I can't wait until we have dozens of huge, clunky scrapbooks stacked in a room with all our crazy memories."

"Hey now. First, let's not age ourselves that quickly. And second, do I really seem like the scrapbooking mom type?"

"Well, okay. We'll have a seriously huge Instagram account then."

"Sounds better. But I agree with you. I'm excited for all the moments, big and small."

He kissed her forehead, and then patted her belly. "Amelia, you are the best thing that's ever happened to me. This baby, too. I've never felt so grounded in my life before, so at peace with where I'm at. I love you more than anything."

"When I got pregnant, I thought it was the worst thing that could ever happen to us. I saw music, our touring as our lives. I thought we had it all. It took a while for me to realize, though, that music is a major part of our lives, but it's just a part. It makes me feel happy and like I'm where I'm supposed to be. But this baby, well, this baby is everything. It makes everything else seem so much smaller, so much less. I can't imagine missing out on this part of life. I know it's going to be hard and take sacrifice, but it's so worth it. I would do anything to feel this love, no matter the cost."

They snuggled in for the night, spending some time talking about more hopes and fears. They talked about their music and where they saw their careers going. They talked about family and friends, about godparents and christenings. They talked until the words became sporadic and their breathing heavy. They talked until they fell asleep in each other's arms, the promises of the future and the love of the romantic weekend lulling them into peaceful dreams.

Chapter Twenty-Seven

Charlotte

"Leonard, can you turn it up? It's hard to hear what Drew is saying in here." Charlotte was doing some dishes after they'd made breakfast together. It was a Friday morning, and Charlotte was filled with nervous energy. She needed to focus on the price of canned goods and items priced at exorbitant rates to keep her mind off her anxiety.

"Got it, dear. Can you hear it?" He turned from his recliner to look at her, and she turned from washing the coffee mug to eye the television.

"It's seven hundred and ninety-two bucks," she screamed, her stomach knotting at the thought. Not many shows could suck her in, but *The Price is Right* always made her feel like she was actually on the show. She was darn good at guessing the prices of odd items, something she took pride in.

"You're way too high. For that watch? Come on," Leonard argued. "One dollar."

She raised an eyebrow at him. "You're on."

"What do I get if I win?" He winked at her.

"A kiss."

"And if I lose?"

"You have to take me to see that new movie."

"The chick flick?"

"Now, just because it's about love doesn't mean it's a chick flick."

"Are there guns, war, or cars in it?" Leonard asked.

"No, not really."

"Then it's a darn chick flick."

"Well, regardless, that's the deal. Take it or leave it."

"That's a different game show."

"Stop arguing. What's happening?" She had lost track of the show due to their incessant bickering. They both turned their attention back to the television to see a contestant running on stage.

"What the heck was the amount?" Charlotte yelled, warm water still running.

"I don't know. You were too busy yammering. I missed it."

"Can't you rewind it using that newfangled thing Amelia set up?"

"That TVR?"

"I think it's DVR, dear."

"Well, what button is it?"

"The little stop-sign-looking thing?"

Leonard pushed a button. An odd, multi-colored menu came up.

"Nope. Not it."

"The little arrow?"

Leonard pushed another button. Now the volume went away.

"No."

"Oh, for God's sake. Just turn it off. I knew that new machine was a terrible idea. The thing is just messing up our television."

"Oh well. I think we've watched enough game shows this week, anyway. We need to get out of here."

"Oh, my. I guess no one wins the bet."

"Well, I guess I'll just have to steal my winnings."

He hobbled over to her with his cane. She turned back to her dishes.

"You didn't win. No kiss."

"Oh, come on. I know better. You can't resist my charm."

She smiled in spite of herself, turning to face him. She put the dish down and turned the water off. "Oh, you're right. Come here," she said, pulling his face to hers and kissing him gently. "So what do you want to do once I finish these?"

"I figured you'd want to go see Amelia."

"Well, I do. I want to tether myself to the girl, truth

be told. But Annie told me to stay away, to give Owen and Amelia some privacy until it's time. I suppose she's right. But I'm telling you, the second I get the phone call, the moment that girl is admitted, we're there. I don't care if it takes ninety-eight hours of labor, we're staying until my grandbaby is born."

"So you're saying we're going to go eat lunch in the hospital cafeteria just in case Amelia gets taken in today?"

"Well, that isn't a bad idea…."

"Listen, why don't we do lunch, but how about instead of the hospital cafeteria, we choose something near the hospital. That way, we don't contract Ebola unnecessarily from eating germ-infested, gloppy hospital food. But, if Amelia goes into labor, we won't be too far away."

Charlotte finished up the last dish, dried her hands, and looked at him. "Yeah, you're right. Not a bad idea. Let's go to that old café in town. It's close, and I could go for some chicken and dumplings. Plus, afterward, as long as Annie doesn't call of course, we could head to the mall for another shirt for baby Charlotte. I need something to go with those adorable pink sparkly pants I found."

"You do realize the spare bedroom looks like a baby store already, right?"

"Leonard, don't you lecture me about buying too much stuff. A girl can never have too many clothes, no matter what her age."

"That's what you said yesterday when we went and

got five more outfits."

"Well, it's the truth."

Leonard laughed, shaking his head.

"What?"

"You. You're always worrying about everyone else."

"Will you stop complaining about that?"

"I'm not complaining. I think it's beautiful. But aren't you tired? Don't you ever just want to slow down?"

"There'll be time for that. When I'm dead."

"Oh, Charlotte. Never one to mince words."

She softened, leaning into his arms. "I'm so glad everything is working out."

"Me, too. I love you."

"I love you too."

She looked at him. "Well, we've got a while until lunch. Do you want to go on the patio for some coffee? Maybe roust up Bridget?"

"Sounds great. Do you want to take your phone?"

Charlotte looked at him like he was the silliest man on earth. She pulled the cell phone—Amelia had called it a smartphone, but Charlotte felt anything but smart when she used it—out of her pants. "Obviously," she said, tucking the phone back in her pants. She had made Annie check it yesterday to make sure the volume was on high and to run through a tutorial with her again on how to answer a call. She was still getting the hang of it. She did have to admit, though, it was nice being able to leave the apartment even when she was waiting to hear from someone.

"Let's go, then," Leonard said, ushering her to the door.

Charlotte told him to wait a minute. She headed to the Keurig, making three cups of coffee before they left. She seriously considered spiking her coffee with some Baileys, just to calm her nerves, of course.

As she was pondering whether or not she'd drunk the last of the Baileys from Christmastime or if it was still in her cupboard, a loud noise echoed through the apartment.

It was the theme from *The Hunger Games.*

"What in God's name?" Leonard asked.

"My phone!" Charlotte shrieked, abandoning the coffee to pull the phone out of her pocket. "It's ringing. What do I do?"

"Answer it," Leonard ordered.

"Right, of course." Her hands were shaking. She could see Annie's name on the screen. This was it. This was the big moment she'd been waiting for. Things had begun.

Her fingers jiggled the keys. Nothing happened. She swiped on the screen, but nothing happened. She poked and prodded, trying to remember which symbol did what on the screen.

Her anger grew, and just as she was ready to bash the phone to pieces…

It stopped ringing.

"Darn it. I missed the call. Now what?"

They stared at each other, a moment of indecision. Then, at the same exact time, they both just said, "Let's go."

"Hospital food it is," Charlotte said, heading to Marla's door to tell her the news. After rousting Marla from her nap, helping her find her keys, and getting her dressed, the three of them headed downstairs, Leonard hobbling to the car. Neither Leonard nor Charlotte really liked to drive anymore and it was frowned upon with their individual health issues, but neither cared today. They were not waiting for a transport bus.

Although, at the rate Leonard was going, it might've been faster to call the bus.

"It better not be a short labor," Charlotte said, wringing her hands in nervousness. She could not miss this.

"I feel like that's something you should not say to Amelia," Leonard added, chuckling.

Charlotte hit him. "Don't make jokes at a time like this. Things are serious. My great-granddaughter's coming. And I want to make sure everyone is safe and healthy."

Sliding into the passenger seat, Charlotte felt the sun light her face. She closed her eyes, rocking slightly, chanting, as she buckled herself in. Marla was already climbing into the backseat.

"Are you praying?" Leonard asked, clutching her hand. She simply nodded.

"Patron saint of pregnant women?"

She shook her head, still chanting a religious monologue, her lips barely moving.

"Patron saint of fertility? Of health?"

She opened her eyes to look at him. "Fertility?

Really?"

"Well, I was just curious."

"If you must know, I'm praying to Charlie. I figure he might have an in with the big man, so he can help pass along my prayer for me."

Leonard just nodded, patting her hand.

"Wait, Leonard, you're not mad right?"

"Why would I be?"

"About Charlie. Me praying to him."

"Stop being foolish, and keep praying. From what I've heard, labor is no picnic. Amelia needs all the help she can get. If that is her grandfather, so be it."

Charlotte nodded, squeezing his hand, and went back to her chant.

Please Charlie, let them both live, let them both be okay. Watch over them. I'll do anything for them to make it through. I'll even be nice to Catherine. Please Charlie, let them both live, let them both be okay....

***

"Leonard, hurry up, come on," Charlotte ordered, shuffling her feet quickly on the sidewalk, her rosary clutched in her hand. Leonard steadied his cane and then hurried to catch up, Marla by his side.

Although "hurried" wasn't ever really a part of either Marla or Leonard's vocabulary. He methodically plodded along, the cane in one hand. Marla also sauntered along, a smile on her face showing she was also thrilled for this baby.

Charlotte reminded herself to breathe. These things

took time. That baby could stay in a little longer.

Once inside the hospital, Charlotte involuntarily shuddered. The last time she'd been here, things hadn't been going her way. She'd had the stroke and had left there for the nursing home. It was rough.

This, however, was a joyous occasion. Charlotte was worried for Amelia and her namesake. But as long as everything went well, she could soon be holding her first great-grandbaby. She couldn't wait.

They made their way to the front desk, where they got directions. After an elevator ride, an argument with Leonard about the floor number, and picking up a few bemused elevator riders on the floors on the way up, they made it to the maternity wing.

As soon as they got to the waiting room, Charlotte spotted Annie, anxiously pacing. Joe was nearby, resting in the waiting room seats, looking worn out already. Beside him was Jocelyn, the fourteen-year-old Annie and Joe were fostering. Over the holidays, the two had announced their decision to plunge into parenthood by fostering. Now their announcement was reality, with Jocelyn arriving a few months ago. Charlotte couldn't be happier. The more the merrier, as they always said— well, except when it came to Catherine. That was a piece of the family she could let go of.

Snapping back to what mattered now—that precious granddaughter and great-grandbaby, of course— Charlotte hurried toward her daughter.

"Annie?"

"Mom," Annie replied, relief on her face. "I'm so glad you're here."

"Is everything all right?"

Annie nodded, embracing Charlotte, then pulling back to talk to her. "So far, yes. But things are progressing quickly. She's already at eight centimeters!"

"Eight? Already? Is that bad? Are the doctors worried?"

"What the heck does eight centimeters mean?" Leonard asked, scratching his head.

"It means the cervix—" Annie started, sounding like a medical commercial.

"What service? What? Charlotte, what's happening?" Marla asked, confused as usual. Annie and Charlotte eyed each other awkwardly, neither wanting to mime what Annie had just said for the hard-of-hearing Marla. They just smiled and nodded, hoping the question would go away. Before they had time to worry about playing charades with the word "cervix," Leonard spoke up.

"Okay, enough," Leonard replied, throwing his hands in the air. "I'm going to go sit with Joe. You can talk about your lady things. Just let me know if you need anything." Marla, still looking quizzical, decided to follow Leonard to a seat, apparently content being kept in the dark.

Charlotte couldn't help but chuckle. But then she was quickly back to being serious. "Did you see her?"

"Yeah."

"And? How's she holding up?"

"Like a woman in labor. Let's just say Owen looks

scared to death. She's pretty upset right now."

"She'll pull through. She's strong. Did she get an epidural?"

"Hell no. Of course not. That difficult child always takes a challenge. Although this time, I think she's reevaluating the option to take on a natural childbirth. I felt awful for her, in so much pain. But I'm so excited too. I can't wait to hold that baby."

"I'm guessing those two wanted to be in the delivery room alone?"

"Amelia didn't say anything, and it killed me to leave, but I thought they deserved their privacy. This is a big moment for them. I didn't want to make it about me."

Charlotte nodded, and the two headed to take a seat, headed to play the waiting game, to wait for Owen to tell them their new family member had arrived.

This was definitely a better hospital trip than last time.

Chapter Twenty-Eight

Annie

When Annie first had arrived at the hospital and learned how quickly labor was going for Amelia, she was relieved. First, she was relieved her daughter might not have to endure the twenty-eight-hour labor she had dealt with. Second, she was thrilled she would have her granddaughter in her arms sooner rather than later.

Now, though, things seemed to be slowing down. Annie kept checking at the desk, asking if there was any progress. But this baby, who had been seemingly in a hurry before, was now taking her time coming into the world. Amelia was still not dilated enough to push.

Annie couldn't help but think about how, decades ago, she had been the one in Amelia's shoes, praying for labor to be done, screaming at Dave for being an asshole and getting her pregnant, and, after it was all done, being madly in love with him when she saw her beautiful baby girl.

Motherhood had changed her. Suddenly, in one moment, nothing else mattered other than that soft, warm baby in her arms. She knew this was about to happen for Amelia too.

She'd already seen so many changes in her daughter. There was truly that pregnancy glow about her, but there was something more. This baby had grounded her not so much in reality as in what she wanted. The baby had helped Amelia see that a life of love and family wasn't a boring life at all, or at least it didn't have to be. The baby forced Amelia to open her eyes to the amazing life in front of her.

Annie was grateful for that.

Sure, there would be difficult moments of confusion and sacrifice. Annie knew there would be phone calls over the next weeks and months about bath water temperatures and diaper rashes and all sorts of crazy situations. But she couldn't wait to share every one of them with her daughter. Mercifully, despite the pull of traveling and the open road, Amelia had settled in, had stayed close to her. She couldn't be happier about that.

Annie's thoughts were quickly interrupted as a familiar—and, truthfully, uncomfortable—sight flashed into the waiting room.

Dave.

"How is she?" he muttered, clearly panicked. Sweat

was rolling off his forehead in a rather unattractive way.

"She's in labor. How the heck do you think she is?" Charlotte sarcastically spat, and Annie gave her a scowl. She stood to walk toward Dave. Owen must have called him. Apparently Amelia had decided to include her father, despite their differences. Maybe she realized this was a big moment and, mistakes or not, Dave deserved a chance with his grandchild. Maybe the mothering hormones were softening her attitude toward him. More than that, Annie suspected Owen had something to do with Amelia's inclusive attitude toward her father. Not that Annie was upset about that. He was Amelia's father. They all needed to move on from the past. He had every right to be here.

It just was going to make this waiting room situation a little stranger. Annie glanced at Joe, whose face already had tensed and showed some lines on his forehead. There were no Christmastime libations to ease the tension between them today.

"She was progressing quickly, but it's slowed down now. We're hoping in the next few hours or so, Charlotte will be here in the world with us."

Dave smiled. "How's Amelia doing?"

"She's okay. In a lot of pain. You know our daughter, always taking the difficult route."

"Don't tell me she decided to do it naturally."

"Of course she did. Although I do think she's regretting it now."

"Well, I'm going to sit in the waiting room on the

other end of the hallway. Come get me if there's news?"

Annie was ready to say sure, thinking it was probably a good idea for her ex-husband and her new husband to be in separate corners.

Just as she was about to say that, though, a loud honking noise startled her, and she jumped. She turned to peek past Joe at the entrance to the waiting room.

It was Janie, decked out in a "World's Best Aunt" shirt, a party hat, and tooting a party horn.

"Who's ready to meet a baby?" she proclaimed, wearing her doctor's coat. Annie remembered that she'd been working here in the ER. It hadn't even crossed her mind she'd be on duty. Janie passed out some party horns and hats to the family. Charlotte eyed her suspiciously.

"Dear, I appreciate your zest. But do you think this is appropriate?"

"Of course it is! I've been seeing broken limbs and death all day down in the ER. It's my lunch, so I thought it would be good to come celebrate with you guys. I mean, after all, it is a pretty big thing to celebrate, huh? My big brother's going to be a dad. And that means I'm going to be an aunt. So let's celebrate!" She honked her horn again. A nurse gawked at her, rolling her eyes.

Annie didn't know Janie all that well, but she could tell the girl wasn't your typical stiff-collared doctor. No wonder Amelia loved her so much.

"Anyway, I'm going to go say hi to Owen and get an update. Perk of the coat. I'll get you some updates." She gave Annie a thumbs-up and skipped off to find Owen.

Annie couldn't help but laugh.

"That girl's a doctor?" Jocelyn asked. No one responded, but they were certainly all thinking it.

Dave was standing awkwardly in place, still taking in the scene.

"Well, I'm going to get going over to the room," he said again.

"Listen, Dave, why don't you stay. Janie's right. This is a big moment. You're family, whether I like it or not. Just stay," Joe said, always the selfless one.

Annie turned to face Joe, who hadn't got up from his seat. He gave her a smile, and Annie went over to take her seat by him. Dave nodded, hesitated, and then headed to an empty seat beside Charlotte.

"Thank you," Annie whispered to her husband. She really was lucky to have a man with such a big heart.

Sitting there, glancing around at her loved ones, it suddenly hit Annie. There was someone missing. Just as she was turning to ask Joe if he'd talked to Catherine yet, Annie heard another noise. God, the nurses were probably ready to ban the entire lot of them from the hospital.

"I'm here, I'm here! Damn bus driver was running late," Catherine proclaimed, making her grand entrance.

There was a gasp from Charlotte, and it took Annie a second to understand why.

Catherine wasn't wearing her fancy fur or her gorgeous designer silk shirt. She didn't have on her cashmere sweater or her $500 silk scarf.

Instead, she was wearing something completely un-Catherine, something that would typically be deemed beneath her.

She wore a plain white sweatshirt, probably a simple cotton blend, the kind found on a cheap sale rack at a department store.

This, however, wasn't the reason behind the gasp. It was what was emblazoned on the front of the white sweatshirt.

In glittering hot pink letters, garish enough to be seen a mile away, were the words "World's Greatest Great-Grandma."

It may have just been in Annie's mind, but she could have sworn at that moment she heard a Pitbull song playing in the background. Annie prayed this truly wouldn't be a dance aerobics replay.

***

Joe leaped from his seat. "Mother, how are you? Why don't you come sit over here?" He motioned her toward the far end of the waiting room, way out of Charlotte's range.

"There is a waiting room at the other end of the hospital, if you'd like. I've heard they have a better vending machine," Charlotte added, sarcasm oozing from her words.

"Oh, no, dear. I'll sit right by you. But first, I have something for Charlotte and for Marla."

Annie eyed Joe suspiciously. Things had definitely been better between Catherine and Charlotte, but they were still waiting for it to crash and burn.

Joe shrugged as his mother walked over to Charlotte and pulled something out of her tote bag.

Charlotte paused, but took the item from Catherine, unbunching it.

It was a "World's Greatest Great-Grandma" sweatshirt, identical to Catherine's. Catherine handed Marla one, too. Annie smiled, realizing maybe the peace wasn't so tenuous after all.

"So we're going to be twinning?" Charlotte asked, giving Catherine a look.

"Well, yes, I will stoop to your fashion level for just one day. I was going to get this embroidered on cashmere, but I knew your backwards self wouldn't know how to handle such a high quality fabric. So I went to the Walmart instead."

"It's just Walmart. There's no *the* in the name."

"Whatever, you old bag. Just be happy I'm agreeing to match you. I figured it's for a good cause."

"Ladies, please. Catherine, this was a lovely gesture. Thank you. And Mom, you should probably thank her, right? Because it was a lovely gesture."

"If you say so. Thanks, Catherine, for this gaudy sweatshirt. It's just stunning." She bit into the last word. However, she put the sweatshirt on over her shirt anyway. Annie detected a hint of a smile. The shirt might be flashy, but she knew the words on it meant more to Charlotte than outwitting Catherine.

They sat, all chattering. Jocelyn talked with Joe and

Leonard about the trip she'd just taken and the new friend she'd made. Catherine and Charlotte bickered—only slightly, which was an improvement—over the latest shuffleboard tournament. Janie popped back in to talk animatedly with all the family members, talking about her shift in the ER and asking about Jocelyn.

Looking around, Annie was taken aback again by this hodgepodge of a family she was now a part of. They were quirky, they didn't always see eye to eye, but they were, in fact, a family. This group of all ages, of all personalities, had somehow found each other and fit together. It was an oddly beautiful thing.

The thought, however, wasn't as beautiful to Annie as the words coming out of Owen's mouth when he popped into the waiting room twenty minutes later.

"She's here!" he said, gasping for breath, looking like he'd just finished an Iron Man.

The whole room erupted into cheers, and Annie even blew on her party horn.

The group floated out of the waiting room simultaneously, the mob of family heading down the hallway to peek at their new family member.

She's already surrounded by love, Annie thought. No matter how much this group of people fought and bickered, no matter how many crazy situations they got themselves into, Annie knew without a doubt they would always be there for this little girl, every single one of them.

Charlotte Grace didn't know it yet, but she was a very blessed little girl.

Chapter Twenty-Nine

Amelia

Resurrected.

That's how Amelia felt when she saw those baby blue eyes, felt the warm skin of Charlotte Grace in her arms after hours of labor.

From a physical standpoint, she truly did feel like she'd come back from the morgue. Her body was weary, more exhausted than it'd ever felt. For a long while in the midst of the most intense labor, she thought she was going to die.

What had she been thinking, choosing natural childbirth?

Owen, of course, had been there, squeezing her hand,

rooting her on, singing to her to take her mind off the pain. His deep eyes were the only thing keeping her going. That and the thought of finally meeting her daughter.

Charlotte Grace resurrected her in other ways, though, too. Suddenly, for the first time in her life, Amelia felt completely grounded in what her life was all about. The songwriting, the money, the house, the cars... nothing meant anything anymore. All that mattered were those seven pounds, six and a half ounces in her arms.

Her world had completely started over.

"She's got your nose," Owen said, eying his new daughter with tears in his eyes.

"She's got your chin," Amelia said. In the past, she'd never understood how anyone could see these things in a wrinkly newborn. They all looked the same to her.

Not anymore.

"I don't think she has my ears, though." Owen smiled, reaching over Amelia to stroke Charlotte's cheek.

"Well, thank God for that, huh?" Amelia played with Charlotte's finger.

Owen leaned down to kiss Amelia.

"I'm so happy. This is the best day of my life," he said. It was a cheesy statement, but in that moment, there was absolutely nothing cheesy about it. Amelia felt the same exact way.

"You should probably go and rally the troops," Amelia said, her eyes feeling heavy. "I'm sure they're dying to meet the newest addition."

"Charlotte Grace has no idea what's coming her way."

Amelia smiled. "Hopefully Grandma and Catherine don't kill each other trying to be the first to see her."

"I'm sure there have already been enough arguments to drive the waiting room crazy. I'll go tell them the news, and then I'll be right back."

He kissed her again, and Amelia closed her eyes, smiling.

As the door to her room closed, she realized how content she felt. A tear trickled down her cheek, the overpowering emotions of the day catching up to her now that she was alone.

Eight months ago, tears had fallen over Charlotte Grace, but they had been of a different type. It was hard to believe there was a time Amelia felt this baby would ruin everything, a time she'd sobbed at the thought of being a mom.

It was hard to believe she'd considered walking away from Owen, considered he might want something more than this.

The past months had been riddled with doubt and confusion as they tried to piece together a life neither had expected. They had waded through waters of uncertainty and confusion, trying to decide if their commitment was strong enough for this. There had been times when she'd wondered if their love could survive this life-changing event. There were moments when she'd felt like their love was gone. There were moments when she'd questioned where their love went.

With clarity now, Amelia realized their love hadn't

actually gone anywhere. It had been there the whole time, cementing the fact they were the real deal.

They had found the solidity of their love in each other's arms, in shared dreams, and in the eyes of Charlotte Grace.

What started as a random kiss over some appetizers had matured into a shared life dream, a desire to make memories, and a love strong enough to carry them and their daughter through this life together.

Chapter Thirty

Charlotte
Six Months Later

The yellow suitcases sat by the door, and Charlotte smiled at them, a nervous, giddy energy exploding in her chest. She had combed through the contents two times last night, making sure she had everything she needed.

The phone rang. It was Annie. "Mom, do you have everything? Passports? Medicines? I just want to make sure you're ready for tomorrow. I have to pick you guys up around four so we can get to the airport on time."

"Yes, dear. Everything's ready. I still can't believe we're going out of the country for this."

"I know. It's so exciting, right?"

"I'll see you tomorrow," she said. "I love you." She

hung up to go finish last-minute preparations. She had to check and make sure Catherine and Marla were also ready for the week ahead. Plus, she had to check in with Henrietta down the hallway and make sure she could still feed Horace and Cheese Curl, their newest addition. Luckily, there was no more hiding of the pets, so she didn't have to worry about that. True to her word—for once—Catherine had brought up the pet situation at the residents' meeting a few months ago. She'd threatened a lawsuit, gotten petitions signed, and fought the no-pets rule.

And that stubborn, usually good-for-nothing woman had won. Charlotte could've kissed her. But then she'd come to her senses.

So now Wildflower Meadows was looking a bit like a zoo. From the time the rule was lifted, everything from birds to cats to tiny dogs were making their way in. Although Catherine had been the one to get the ban lifted, she quickly started complaining that there were now too many mangy animals inside.

That woman would never be content.

All that mattered, though, was that Horace and Cheese Curl were free to stay, and Charlotte didn't have to worry about the cats being let out of the bag—or apartment—when she was gone on the trip.

She had enough other things to worry about, after all. There was so much to do. *Breathe,* she told herself. *You can't drive yourself to a stroke now.*

Her doctor had already been hesitant about her and

Leonard flying. If one of them had any sort of slipup, they'd be forbidden to go. She would not miss this moment for anything.

***

"How in God's name did this happen?" Catherine complained as she claimed her seat—her seat that was right next to Charlotte.

Charlotte looked to the ceiling of the plane as if the answer were written there. "Seriously?"

Leonard, sitting by the window, let out a chuckle. Charlotte was exhausted already from getting up at three in the morning. Plus, she'd barely slept last night from all the excitement. She'd been looking forward to a relaxing, peaceful flight.

Until she realized she was sitting by Catherine.

"It's not funny," Charlotte said, nudging Leonard. "Eight hours in the air, trapped beside Catherine. Switch seats."

"Sure, Leonard can come sit by a real woman, sounds good to me." Catherine winked.

"Never mind." Charlotte scowled.

"They're going to kill each other," Jocelyn said to Janie. The two girls were seated in the row in front of them.

"Not true," Catherine answered, her fluffy fur coat causing Charlotte to sneeze already. "We can handle being civil now, right, Charlotte?"

Charlotte sneezed again. "Did you have to wear that dang ugly coat?"

"This, I will have you know, is one-of-a-kind fur."

"What? Artificial?"

Catherine gasped. "You just have no class."

"Mom, Catherine, please," Annie scolded from the row behind them.

Charlotte settled in as the Fasten Seat Belt sign came on. She could hear baby Charlotte cooing from a few rows ahead where Amelia and Owen sat. She smiled.

Yes, she could be civil for one flight in order to make this trip perfect for her family. She could do it.

***

"Charlotte, wake up, look," Leonard said, elbowing her. When she came to, she realized she had fallen asleep on Catherine's shoulder.

She'd even drooled a little.

This made Charlotte smile. She left Catherine snoring, her head back in her seat, to turn to Leonard.

"What?"

"Look at the view," he said, pointing to the ground.

All Charlotte could see was green. Green for miles.

"Okay, folks, this is your pilot. Please fasten your seat belts. We will be landing in Dublin shortly."

"Ireland!" Charlotte squealed, waking up Catherine.

Amelia, disobeying the "fasten seat belt" warning, leaned up and over her seat to glance back at her grandma.

"We made it," she said, smiling.

Charlotte started to cry.

They would see Ireland after all. Their dream trip was coming true, only better.

This time her daughter, granddaughter, great-granddaughter, and a handful of other important people in her life would be there to share in the moment.

**

The women huddled in the entrance to the hotel they were staying at while the men unloaded the luggage from the taxis. Charlotte peeked out the tiny window to see Owen and Joe attempting to heave Catherine's bejeweled luggage from the trunk. The woman had probably brought at least five ball gowns just in case.

Turning back to her family, Charlotte saw nothing but smiles. Annie was holding baby Charlotte, making her laugh. It was the most gorgeous sound in the world.

Amelia turned to her. "Are you happy, Grandma?"

"Happy? I'm ecstatic! Honey, you could've been getting married at the local junkyard, and I'd have been happy. But this, well, this is unbelievable. I can't believe you did this," she said, tears threatening again. She reached over to hug Amelia.

"Well, we wanted to do something for you, Grandma. You're always doing so much for us, what with you babysitting baby Charlotte anytime we need."

"Oh stop. That is not a chore, by any means."

"This is true," Annie said, turning from the baby. "If you don't ask her to babysit, she's calling me to see if she can steal one of my days."

Amelia smiled. "Well, regardless, we knew you had your heart set on coming here. And to be honest, so did we. Owen and I had always talked about coming here, so we thought, why not?"

"Well, thank you. This is the most beautiful gift," Charlotte said, meaning it.

"Oh for goodness sake, stop being such a sap," Catherine said. Charlotte gave her the death glare, but decided not to let her ruin this moment.

"I'm so happy for you, Amelia. I can't wait to see that wedding dress of yours. So where is the wedding ceremony taking place?"

"Right here, in the hotel. They have a beautiful ballroom for weddings. It's going to be perfect."

"I have no doubt, honey."

Just then, Owen came into the lobby, hauling one of Catherine's many pieces of luggage.

"Oh, dear, please be careful with that, there are at least five—"

"What? Luxury ball gowns that are just simply one-of-a-kind?" Charlotte interrupted, putting on her best Catherine face.

"Why, no, actually. I was going to say there are at least five luxury scarves in there. The ball gowns are in the black suitcase."

Charlotte rolled her eyes. "How silly of me."

Annie chuckled, dancing around with baby Charlotte. "I hope you don't have the sass of your namesake," she whispered to the baby loudly enough for all to hear.

"You know, some people like my sass, right Leonard?" Charlotte said as her husband strolled through the door, wheeling her suitcase.

"Charlotte! You shouldn't say that word, not in public, even if Leonard does like it," Marla said, alarmed.

Amelia burst out laughing. Leonard looked confused. Charlotte just patted Marla on the shoulder, shaking her head. The hearing aid situation hadn't quite been fixed yet.

"Well, I like both of those," Leonard said, winking.

Charlotte huffed, smacked his arm, grabbed her suitcase, and headed to the front desk to get their room key, marveling at the gorgeous decor and breathing in the Irish air.

Catherine or not, this was going to be amazing.

Chapter Thirty-One

Annie

"There has to be a mistake. I definitely booked six separate rooms. I booked a room for Joe and me, Amelia and Owen, Charlotte and Leonard, Marla and Catherine, Janie and Jocelyn, and then one for Dave. Can you please check our records?"

The redhead at the desk logged back into the computer system to do some searching as the group anxiously stood behind Annie, the two babies starting to fuss.

"I'm sorry, ma'am, but looks like there are only five rooms booked."

"Well, okay, not a problem. Can you just give Dave here a different room? Dave, you don't mind being in a separate area of the hotel, right?" She looked back to her ex-husband, who was holding the fussing Esmerelda and already looking frazzled.

"No, we'll be fine," he said, readjusting the diaper bag. Marla took it off his shoulder to help him out, trying to talk to the baby to calm her.

The redhead, whose name was Marie according to the name tag, typed a few more things in the computer before frowning. "I'm very sorry, ma'am, but we're all booked up."

"Until when?"

"Until two weeks from today. Not a single room or even a cancellation anywhere. But if someone does check out early or cancel, I can put you on the waiting list."

Annie sighed, resting her head in her hands. The group behind her erupted into several conversations, phrases such as "oh no" and "now what" punctuating the confusion.

Annie turned to Joe, who was standing by her side.

Dave stepped forward, the baby still fussing. "Maybe I can find a room somewhere else," Dave said.

Janie stepped forward as well. "Hey, there's a hotel down the street. I could go get a room for Jocelyn and me down there."

One by one, each member of the group stepped forward, offering to go and find another room. Mass confusion ensued.

"Enough!" Annie said, her mind reeling. "Enough. I

appreciate everyone offering to help, but please just give me a second to think."

The group, wide-eyed at Annie's outburst, froze.

Joe was the only one to break the silence. He sighed, an audible, huge gust of air coming from his lungs. "Why don't you just stay with us? Our room has a cot, right?" He turned to the clerk, who answered his question with a yes.

The group now stood open-mouthed, looking at each other.

"Joe, you don't have to do that," Amelia said, stepping forward.

"Don't be silly. We have enough to organize and worry about, with the wedding tomorrow. We don't need everyone scrambling to find another room. It'll be fine. And like Marie said, if something opens up, we'll take it. Until then, just stay with us."

Annie pulled Joe aside, whispering, "Are you sure? This is crazy."

"It'll be fine. Besides, there's a lovely pub downstairs. A few dozen ales, and I won't know the difference." He smiled despite Annie's frown. "I'm kidding. Loosen up."

"Don't you think it'll be awkward?"

He turned back toward Dave, who also stood in silence. Joe slapped him on the shoulder. "Awkward? Me and your ex, sleeping in the same room with you? With his baby girl from another woman? What could possibly be awkward about that?"

Everyone stood still, not making a sound, afraid of

reacting incorrectly.

And then Leonard let out a chuckle. The whole group followed suit.

Marie eyed them all suspiciously, but handed out the room keys. "Enjoy your stay," she said, punctuating it with a questioning tone.

Annie should've known better than to expect things to go smoothly.

This was their lives they were talking about.

She would expect nothing less than having her ex-husband and his baby to his prior mistress sleeping in the room with her and her new husband.

She would expect nothing less at all.

***

"So we really have this place to ourselves?" Joe wrapped his arms around her as she took in the view from their balcony.

"Well, at least until Dave comes wandering back in." Joe kissed her neck, and a shudder ran through her.

"Please don't remind me."

"Hey, mister," she said, turning around and poking his chest, "this was your brilliant idea."

"What was I supposed to do? Shove him on the street? I want this to be perfect for Amelia and Owen. I didn't think they needed any more stress. My mother certainly causes enough of it by herself."

"No arguments there. Was it really necessary for her to request a lemon to put in her bottled water from the mini bar? Oh my."

They smiled, Annie wrapping her arms around his neck. "So, Dave is going to be gone for at least a few hours. Esmerelda and Charlotte Grace are with Janie and Jocelyn down the hall. What do you want to do with ourselves?" She kissed his cheek, hinting at what she thought they should do.

But he surprised her. "I can think of a lot of things we could do. But we *are* in Ireland. What do you say we get a little crazy?"

She raised an eyebrow. "What do you have in mind?"

"Let's go out."

"Really? Like out on the town? We don't even know the area."

"Exactly. Let's get a little lost. Go out, get some drinks. Look, Jocelyn will be fine with Janie. We can afford to have some fun, live a little."

The responsible, mousey Annie from the past told her she shouldn't. She couldn't. There were a million reasons they should stay put. There was Amelia's wedding tomorrow, for starters. She needed to have her *A* game on to make sure everything went just right. There was Jocelyn—what if she needed something? Sure, Janie was an adult, but still….

She contemplated all the rational reasons she shouldn't go out to a pub in the middle of Dublin at this time of night.

Looking into Joe's eyes, though, she saw something else. She saw the Annie he saw, a little less mousey, a lot less rational. A fun-loving, zesty woman he'd fallen for quite literally at Wildflower a few years ago.

They'd been through quite a year. There'd been the overwhelming joy of getting married, of settling in to a life together. There'd been the excitement of falling in love again, in realizing love was still possible. There'd been beautiful moments, stolen kisses, moments of sheer normalcy on the sofa together.

There had been plenty of mistakes, though, too. There'd been plenty of ugly moments, fights, and days she thought it couldn't possibly work out. There'd been days to test their love, days they thought their love had vanished. There were days she thought her past with Dave would always cloud the love she had with Joe. There were days she thought love had, in fact, disappeared for good.

But here they were, still standing, together. They'd made it through the trials, the tests, the questions, the confusion, and they were together, still in love. Their love hadn't gone away. It had stayed strong, steadfast, and ready to carry them through life as long as they were willing to hold on to it. They were still together, still crazy about each other, still better because of each other.

So Annie let go of the past, of the rational Annie she would've been with Dave. She said good-bye to the worries and the "what-ifs" and the "I shouldn'ts". She wrapped her arms around her husband's neck, the husband who made her want to be different.

"Blarney me," she said.

"What?"

"I don't know. I was trying to use the Irish slang. When in Rome?"

Joe just eyed her.

"Damn it, Joe. I'm saying fine, let's go out and have some fun."

His smile grew, he kissed her, ushered her toward the door and said, "After you."

***

A few hours and a few strong beverages later, they decided to make their way to the front of the bar, where a band was playing. There were a few horrible attempts at an Irish jig, some loud laughter, and some tripping. There were more strong beverages. There was more dancing. Annie's head started to feel funny… so she had a few more beverages.

Then it happened.

Annie saw a guy eying her from across the bar. He seemed to be watching them.

Or at least that's what Annie thought.

"That guy is going to steal our money," she said loudly, just as the band came to a break in the song. Everyone in the bar turned to see who she was talking about.

"Annie, what?" Joe said, looking around to see the imminent danger.

"That guy over there. He's staring at us. He knows we're tourists. Oh my God, he's going to rob us and then leave us in a ditch. I knew we shouldn't have come here."

Joe put an arm around her. "Annie, calm down. I think the alcohol is just hitting you. It's fine."

"No, it's not. He's going to rob us!" she shrieked, the fear becoming uncontrollable.

Suddenly, the guy approached them.

"See, here he comes. Now do you believe me?" She felt Joe's arm tense.

"He probably heard you, Annie. Now you pissed him off."

The guy came toward them, stoic and muscular. Annie froze. This was it. This was where they became a newspaper headline in the States tomorrow—American Couple Murdered in Quaint Irish Pub Night Before Daughter's Wedding.

"Hello, lad, is there a problem?" the guy said. Annie paused. Lad? That didn't sound too badass or robber like.

"No, we're fine."

"Great. I'm Clancy. This is my pub. Your missus just looked upset. Wanted to make sure no one was bothering her."

Annie felt her face fall. She wanted to die of embarrassment.

It was, in fact, the alcohol talking. She knew she was a paranoid drunk. Now so did Clancy.

"Everything's great," she said, trying to shield the embarrassment. "My daughter's getting married tomorrow, so we should be going."

"Tell the lass congrats," Clancy said before turning around.

Annie pulled Joe on the walk of shame.

In the Irish air, Joe started to chuckle. "Be careful. We

might end up in a ditch on the way home. That Clancy is a real badass."

"Shut up. He looked scary."

They stumbled hand in hand back to the hotel, Annie hoping she could walk off some alcohol and shame.

***

"Shh, Joe, you're being loud," Annie said, snorting through the words. The hotel was quiet, and the lights were out. She tripped over the carpet in the hallway as she followed Joe to their room.

"I'm not the one being loud," he whispered. "You're going to wake the whole floor."

"I think those beers were a little strong."

"We *are* in Ireland."

She found this uproariously funny.

Oh, God, she thought. *I did have too many.* She was feeling buzzed. Suddenly, she started to panic. As she continued following Joe to their room, she frantically pulled on his arm.

"Joe, what am I going to do? I drank way too much and now I'm going to be a mess tomorrow for Amelia's wedding! This was a terrible idea." She suddenly felt like crying.

Joe stopped, turning to talk to her. "You're going to be fine. You didn't have that much."

"I feel like I did."

"It's not that late. Listen, you're going to go in our room and rest. The wedding isn't until two. You'll be fine."

She started to breathe again. Joe was right. Thank God for him.

"Sorry. You're right. I just get a little…."

"Paranoid when you're drinking? I know. Trust me, I know."

She winced. "Sorry. That guy in the bar just looked shady."

"Clearly."

Annie sighed. Just her luck. She tried to have one night of fun… and she ended up insulting the owner of the Irish pub while also getting totally drunk. Tomorrow was going to be a long day. She hoped there was some strong coffee brewing in the lobby.

Before she could think about it anymore, she collapsed onto the covers, her head and body succumbing to the wobbly world of drunken sleep.

***

"Mom, get up. Get up. I need some help. Grandma Charlotte forgot to pack her gown, and now we need to find one. Like now. Can you go help her?"

Annie's head was pounding. Was she dreaming? She was so confused. As her eyes peeked open, a weird sunlight cascading in, she glanced up at Amelia.

Recognition set in.

She tried to sit up quickly, worried she'd overslept from a night of jigging and Irish ale.

"What time is it?" she said, one eye squinting. She ran a hand through her hair. It was a disaster.

"Mom, were you drinking last night?" Amelia inquired.

She looked at her daughter, not sure how to best respond. Suddenly, she heard a familiar snoring. That lip-smacking snoring that had driven her crazy for over a decade.

She peeked around Amelia, seeing the familiar man in the bed beside her and Joe's.

That was right. Dave had spent the night in their room. She involuntarily shuddered again at how weird the situation was. Oh well, at least they'd survived.

"Mom? Hello? Can you please help out? Grandma Charlotte's freaking out, Owen's with the baby right now, and Jocelyn and Janie are driving me crazy wanting to do my makeup already. The priest is checking in with us every few minutes making sure everything's okay, and the hotel staff wants to know about centerpieces. I'm going to snap."

Annie shook off the hangover, knowing she'd have to muster through. "It's going to be fine, honey. Breathe. Just give me ten minutes to pull myself together, and I'll go help Grandma. You just focus on you."

Beside her, Joe stirred. "Tell her to borrow one from my mom," he said, even though his eyes were still closed.

Amelia and Annie simultaneously snorted.

"You can be the one to suggest that to my mom," Annie said while Amelia shook her head.

"Oh Lord, I can only imagine."

"Maybe, though....," Annie said, tapping her chin. "Maybe if she doesn't know it came from Catherine...."

"You really think you're going to get Catherine to

agree to that? Plus, do you think Catherine is going to have a gown that isn't, well, Catherine?"

Annie sighed. "You're right. Maybe you should break the news to Charlotte. If you could pull out some fake tears, Charlotte would go for just about anything."

"I'm not manipulating Grandma."

"It's not manipulating, per se. It's just, well, it's just persuading her lightly."

"No."

"Oh, fine. Then I will take your eighty-two-year-old grandma shopping in Ireland for a dress for your wedding. Why not."

"Do you want to take my mother with you?" Joe said, peering at her over the comforter this time.

She punched him in the arm. "Keep up it, and I'll send you with both of them."

"I love you, but not that much."

She started tickling him.

"Okay, this is getting weird. I'm leaving."

Suddenly, a thought struck Annie. "Hey, how did you get in here anyway?"

"Um, you guys left the door open."

"Oh my God, did we?" Annie was horrified.

"No, Mom, of course you two weren't out drinking last night," Amelia said sarcastically. She then looked at her father on the bed behind them. "I'm sorry, the three of you. This room has too much weirdness for me. I'm going back over to my groom-to-be and my daughter. Please help Grandma sort out the dress thing. Come over to my room when you're done so we can get ready then, okay?"

Annie got out of bed, still wearing last night's clothes. They reeked of alcohol. "Honey, things are going to be fine. Don't worry about anything, okay? I love you. I'll take care of everything."

"As long as you keep the ale away from her," Joe mumbled.

Amelia just shook her head, exiting the room.

Annie headed to the bathroom to get a look at herself, gasped, and then prayed she'd be able to find a salon with a makeup artist while she was out scouring Dublin's shops for a dress.

Chapter Thirty-Two

Amelia

Amelia sat on the bench by the small vanity in the corner of the room, Charlotte on her lap cooing softly. She kissed her baby's head then looked into the mirror, staring back at her reflection.

In spite of everything she saw, all the flaws, she smiled.

Today, she would marry him. She would officially seal their perfect little family.

Not that she needed this formality to make their family real. Holding baby Charlotte, love surged in her veins. Their life might be chaotic, might be far from the life she'd once imagined.

But it was perfect to her.

There'd been so many changes over the past six months. There'd been Owen rejoining the band, although on a very limited schedule. He'd only gone to one venue so far, but the light in his eyes when he'd returned had made it worth missing him. She hoped in the coming months as she settled in to her new role, she'd be able to join him—although, in truth, traveling with a baby wasn't as easy as she'd thought.

For now, songwriting had flown to the backburner, Charlotte taking up every second of Amelia's thoughts. Late-night feedings, early morning frantic searches for keys and baby bottles and diaper pads. There'd been exhaustion like she'd never experienced before. It was a lot to adjust to and, sometimes, more than she thought she could handle. There'd been moments when she wanted to cry right along with Charlotte.

Through all the questions and struggles, though, one thing remained constant.

Owen.

Even on days when it felt like everything was falling apart or when she doubted herself as a mom, he was right there beside her, making her laugh. He made her smile when things got unbearable. He soothed her when she felt like she'd made a mistake.

He made her feel happy even when they were simply sitting on the sofa basking in a moment of quiet when Charlotte was taking a nap.

It had taken a baby and settling down for Amelia to

realize life never truly calmed down, not with Owen. It would never be stale or boring or washed up. It would just *be*.

"Hey, beautiful," Owen said, kissing Amelia as he snuck up behind her. "You ready to do this?" He reached for Charlotte, and she passed the baby to him. The baby instantly started smiling. Owen was a natural.

"I guess," she said, grinning.

"Do you hear your mommy? She's a jerk sometimes, huh?" he said to the baby, mocking Amelia.

"You better get out of here, you know. Everyone already thinks we've doomed our relationship by spending the night before our wedding together."

He laughed. "Pretty sure we've already broken all the conventions."

"Agreed. But I don't feel like hearing Grandma Charlotte and Catherine harping on me about how I wasn't supposed to see you on my wedding day."

"All right, all right. I'll go hang out with Joe or Dave."

"Okay. Can you get your sister? I suppose I should start getting ready soon."

He nodded, then paused to look at her. "I love you, Amelia."

"I love you too."

He leaned down and kissed her, pulling back to say, "The next time we kiss, we'll be stuck together forever."

"Unless we get divorced," she said practically.

He laughed again. "You're ridiculous. What a hopeless romantic."

"I'm kidding. You're never getting rid of me."

"Good."

He headed out, and Amelia found herself grinning long after he'd gone.

Yes, things with Owen were perfect in a completely imperfect way.

***

"We have so much work to do," Janie exclaimed as she breezed into Amelia's room.

"We do?" she asked. Amelia hadn't really been rattled yet. Her mom was out dealing with the dress situation with Grandma Charlotte. Everything else was taken care of. Her appearance was the last worry on her list. She personally didn't care if she wore jeans.

"Your hair needs to be done, your makeup needs to be fixed. We've got to get working," Janie said, pulling out a bag of supplies.

"You came prepared," Amelia observed.

"I *am* maid of honor. That's my job. Now sit."

"Yes, ma'am." Amelia obeyed, sitting down and letting Janie get to work.

"Where's your mom and grandma?"

"They should hopefully be back any minute. They went out with Catherine to find Charlotte a new dress."

"That sounds like a disaster."

"Probably."

"So are you ready for this?"

"Absolutely."

"I don't want to get all sappy on you, but I'm so glad

Owen found you. You're perfect for him."

"Thanks. I'm glad, too. I never thought I'd be the type to settle in with a family. But everything just feels so right."

"That's because it is."

Amelia turned to look at her soon-to-be sister-in-law.

"Thank you for doing this for me."

"What? Your hair? You haven't seen it yet. Save your thank-yous."

"Not my hair. Being in the wedding."

"Where else would I be?"

"I wish your parents could be here too. I wish I could've met them."

Janie got a faraway look in her eyes.

"I'm so sorry. That was a dumb thing to say," Amelia said, feeling herself blush.

"No, no. It's fine. It's a perfectly normal thing to say. It's just I was thinking the same thing. Amelia, they would've loved you. They'd be so happy Owen found you. Mom was so much like your mom. They could've been sisters. I miss her and Dad so much."

Amelia patted Janie's arm as she continued to work on her hair.

"So I guess this is a perfect segue." Janie handed Amelia the curling iron. "Hold this a second."

She went to rustle in the bag beside her until she pulled out a small silver-wrapped box. "Here. It's for you."

"You didn't have to get me anything."

"Just open it."

Amelia did, carefully undoing the paper and bow. Inside the box, she found a pair of earrings. They were black diamonds cut in a triangular shape. They were completely gorgeous, and completely Amelia.

"I love them, Janie. They're perfect! They're so me."

"I know. I saw them and thought of you right away."

"Thank you, but they're too much."

"They were my mom's." Janie paused, eying Amelia with a smile and tears.

"Janie, I can't," she said.

"Yes, you can. Mom would want you to have them. It'll be like a piece of her passes on. Someday you'll give them to my beautiful niece, and they'll continue in the family."

"Janie, don't you want to keep them? To pass on to your children?"

Janie shook her head. "I want you to have them. Seriously. I know you're not into tradition, but they can be your something old."

Amelia hugged Janie, feeling a warmth in her heart. She was truly lucky to not just have Owen in her life, but his amazing sister too. "Thank you. I love them."

With that, the door to Amelia's room flew open again. Amelia could hear bickering already and pulled away from the sentimental moment.

"Grandma? Mom?"

"Amelia! You look… well, interesting at the moment," Charlotte said, eying Amelia's half-done hair.

"No worries. We're still working on it," Janie added,

going back to her work as she swiped at her eyes.

"You're one to talk about appearances. Wait until you see what your grandma is wearing to the wedding," Catherine said, rushing to Amelia's side like a five-year-old ready to tattle to a teacher.

"You old hag, what are you even doing in here? I told you to go back over with Marla and get ready."

"She is my step-granddaughter. I have just as much right to be here."

"Step. As in a step away," Charlotte retorted, rushing to Amelia.

Amelia turned to see her mother walking through the door, looking even worse than she had that morning. Annie plodded over to the chair where Amelia sat as Charlotte and Catherine continued bickering about their outfits.

"Mom?"

Annie said nothing, her head lolling. She looked like hell.

"Mom? Are you okay?"

Annie shook her head. "More than ever, I need some Irish ale. Anyone have any?"

Amelia smiled. "That bad, huh?"

"You have no idea."

Amelia turned to eye the women, still arguing. "I can imagine."

"Ladies, can you please take your argument elsewhere? We've got some hair to finish here. I've got to work on Annie next." Janie shooed them away.

"Well, you better do Charlotte's hair too. With that hideous outfit, she'll need something going for her."

"At least I won't look like I'm on the Titanic."

"I'd rather look like I'm on the Titanic in first class than third class doing the Irish jig."

"Catherine, I'm sure Grandma's outfit is fine."

"Oh, I wouldn't be so sure," Annie added, and Amelia turned.

"Why? Grandma, what did you pick?"

"It's perfectly lovely, dear. Goes right along with the theme."

"The theme? What's the theme?"

"Why, Ireland, of course."

"Grandma, what does an Irish-themed dress look like?"

Catherine, Charlotte, and Annie looked at each other and shrugged.

"I offered to give her one of my ball gowns," Catherine added.

"Which is exactly why I bought the dress in Finnigan's Fashion Outlet."

Amelia sighed. "Grandma, listen. I don't care if you come dressed in a paper bag. I'm just glad you're here. All of you. Seriously. I love you all."

"Someone's getting sentimental," Annie said, tearing up and hugging Amelia.

"Mom, are you crying?"

"No. Maybe. Yes."

"Are you crying because I said I love you or because

of the shopping trip?"

"Both."

Amelia laughed. "Whatever happens or whatever you wear, all that matters is that I'm marrying Owen today and that we're all here, healthy and together. Seriously."

"I'll drink to that," Annie said.

Amelia just gave her a look and turned to see the final touches on her hair.

***

"Are you ready?" Dave asked as he put Amelia's arm on his.

She smiled, glad now Annie had convinced her to let Dave walk her down the aisle. She still hadn't completely forgiven her father for what he'd done, but she realized it was time to let it go. If Joe could accept Dave as a part of their lives, she could certainly accept her father, too. Love had turned out unexpectedly for both her parents, but as an adult, she realized that was often the case with love.

Her simple bouquet of roses was balanced in her steady hand. She'd heard of pre-wedding jitters, but there were none of those. She stood, confident and still, waiting to walk down the aisle in front of her friends and family and pledge her life to Owen.

"Let's do this," she said when the music turned to the song that had sealed it all—the song she'd written with Owen.

Owen's voice resonated through the room as the CD played, and Amelia felt herself getting emotional. It was a full-circle moment, one of those moments in life when everything just made perfect sense. They slowly stepped into the ceremony area, reaching the carpeting of the room as the chorus came on. She stopped for a minute, wanting to take everything in. She wanted to remember this scene for the rest of her life. The soft reds of the roses decorating the room. The warmth of the candlelit space. The sight of her family all around her. The sight of him standing, a beaming smile on his face, at the end of the aisle, Janie holding Charlotte in a perfect yellow flower-girl dress.

It was everything she'd never imagined for her life.

She took the first step toward her entire life on the simple lace aisle runner. She leaned on her dad for support.

The whole room smiled back at her. There was Catherine standing in a floor-length sequined black dress, backless like a celebrity would wear. Marla stood near the front, wearing a simple gray dress typical of her age. Her mom and Joe were in the front row, smiling like they would crack. Jocelyn stood, gangly and unsure, holding Esmerelda.

As Amelia continued to step in her studded black stilettos down the aisle, she caught sight of the person she'd been looking for since she stepped out—other than Owen, of course.

Grandma Charlotte.

There she stood, a vision of Ireland, that was for sure. She wore a plaid dress that looked like a mixture between a traditional Irish kilt and a Catholic schoolgirl jumper. It was hunter green with yellow checks in it. On the lapel of the dress, she wore a huge shamrock pin.

It was quite a sight, but when you added the neon-yellow hat her grandma loved so much, it was quite out of this world.

Amelia smiled, a huge, toothy smile. Grandma Charlotte smiled back.

Amelia knew without a doubt the outfit had been a stab at Catherine. The fact she would turn down one of Catherine's expensive, luxurious gowns for that costume was enough to make Catherine seethe.

Other brides might have been mad at Charlotte for making the wedding a mockery or for wearing it, but not Amelia. She thought it was perfect.

It didn't matter. Like she'd said before, it didn't matter what Charlotte wore. It was just the fact she was there. Amelia got it. Charlotte got it.

That was why she loved her grandma so much.

Amelia glanced down now, her eye catching sight of the gorgeous red peeking out from the white overlay in her knee-length dress. She felt perfect in it. It gave her a boost of confidence, confidence she was feeling now as she made it close to the end of the aisle.

When she finally reached Owen, Dave put her hand in his, and she felt herself shudder. The enormity of the moment coupled with her excitement jolted her back to the present, back to what mattered. She heard her family sit down as she took her place by Owen.

"I love you," she said, as soon as the music had stopped.

He smiled at her. "I love you too." He leaned in then, taking her face in his hands, kissing her with the type of passion one only saw in movies. He kissed her like he was a soldier who'd been away at war for two years or like a spouse who'd just realized his wife was alive after all.

It was a kiss that said so much, a kiss steaming with love.

The crowd laughed. Someone clapped—she thought it was Grandma, but she couldn't be sure.

"Well, are you sure we need a wedding?" the officiant said, and Amelia pulled back to laugh.

"Maybe we could just skip to the good stuff?" Owen said.

"Son, looks like you already have."

Looking into Owen's eyes as he laughed again, she saw everything she needed right in front of her. It had started with a random kiss in front of some appetizers, with some confusion over what she wanted.

Standing at the altar now with the man she would pledge her life to, with a baby behind her who meant the world to her, she knew she'd made the right choice.

Once in her life, not long ago, she'd wondered what would make her truly happy, what she wanted. She'd debated whether safety was worth the sacrifice of passion, whether settling down was what would make her satisfied.

Now, standing there, the truth hit her.

Love wasn't about sacrificing yourself or choosing between two good things.

It was about having it all.

With Owen, Charlotte, and this crazy group sitting in the crowd who had become her family, she truly had everything she'd ever wanted.

It was messy at times. It was never perfect. There were fights and tears and doubts. There was a baby spitting up during the Bible reading and Marla asking Charlotte if the priest had just said "fondue" instead of "I do." There was Grandma Charlotte readjusting her dress noticeably every two minutes, probably because the material looked stiff and scratchy as hell.

Amelia knew there would be plenty more interesting moments in the years to come. There would be hardships and frustrations. There would be times she wanted to walk away from Owen, from the family, from everyone.

But, in exchange for those moments, there were also the beautiful ones. The look in Annie's eyes as she watched her exchange I dos. The smile on Jocelyn's face as she held Esmerelda. The jokes from Janie about lost rings.

The room was filled with quite a mix of people, who had come into each other's lives in sometimes strange and unexpected ways. Wasn't that, though, the excitement of life?

When Owen walked into Grandma Charlotte's apartment that first time, Amelia hadn't even thought she'd see him again. But here she was, a few years later, standing in front of the spiky-haired, tattooed rocker guy pledging her heart to him willingly.

Yes, it had been an unconventional path to get here and an unconventional path that followed. There had been the tour life, the crazy life, the settling-down portion of life. It had been tumultuous and scandalous at times. It had been questionable and worrisome and fear-inspiring. Looking back, though, the road to the altar hadn't been good or bad. It had just, quite simply, been her life.

It had taken a year to find this love, a love she didn't expect. Heck, it had been a love she had fought at the time. It took another year of almost losing his love, of losing sight of themselves, of having to figure out where love went.

But here they stood, wrapped together by passion, love, and the vows they were about to say. As she kissed Owen, her husband, for the first time, she felt her heart leap.

Love was never a guarantee. Sometimes there were doubts and worries, broken hearts and regrets. Sometimes love felt like a cruel joke or an impossibility.

Real love, though, made all those bad moments worth enduring. Real love made the questions worth answering.

As they faced their family for the first time as husband and wife, Amelia came to a realization she'd been searching for.

Despite all the doubts and fears of the past year, their love had always been there. Their love hadn't actually gone anywhere at all.

With that, Amelia and Owen dashed out of the ceremony to the cheers of their family. They ran toward the future as fast as their legs could carry them, hearts sealed in an unbreakable link of wedding vows, promises, passion, and a love that wouldn't disappear.

The End

Acknowledgements

First, I want to thank my parents, my biggest fans and supporters. Dad, you taught me that education was everything; you taught me from the time I could talk that education equaled opportunity. Mom, you taught me to love reading, to always be compassionate, to put others before myself, and that sometimes it's okay to eat ice cream for lunch. You have always been my best friend, and I can't imagine a life without you.

Thank you to Chad, the love of my life. You've been there through so many of my life's milestones. I am so lucky to be married to my best friend and to have a man who has a big heart and sense of humor. You make me laugh when I feel like crying, and you remind me that life's about having fun.

Thank you to Hot Tree Publishing for believing in my works and for helping me make them something I'm proud to share with the world. Thank you, Becky, for having an amazing vision for Hot Tree Publishing that has led to a supportive, family-like feel. The amount of support you give to your authors is truly admirable. I am so honored to call myself a Hot Tree author. Thank you to Olivia for your amazing editing skills. You push me to be a better writer, and I am so thankful for that. Thank you to everyone else at Hot Tree who helped make my story come to life.

I also want to thank all my family and friends who have supported me on this writing journey from the beginning. A special thanks to Grandma Bonnie for always being there to support me at all my events. I love you. Thank you to Christie James, Hannah Hauser, Jamie Lynch, Alicia Schmouder, Kay Shuma, Kelly Rubritz, Lynette Luke, Maureen Letcher, Sandra Cecutti-Corey, and everyone else who has tirelessly supported me. From author events to reading my books to your kind words, you've all played a major role in building my confidence as an author. I am so blessed to have all of you.

Thank you to all of the teachers who have helped me get to where I am today. A special thanks to Diane Vella, Sue Gunsallus, Tom Kunkle, and all of the professors at Mount Aloysius College for shaping my writing journey.

Thank you to all of the readers, authors, and bloggers who have also helped me along the way. I cannot thank you enough for all of your support.

Finally, as always, thank you to my writing buddy and fellow cupcake lover, Henry. When I'm having a bad day and feel like giving up, one look in your soulful eyes reminds me that life is beautiful.

About the Publisher

Hot Tree Publishing opened its doors in 2015 with an aspiration to bring quality fiction to the world of readers. With the initial focus on romance and a wide spread of romance sub-genres, they envision opening up to alternative genres in the near future.

Firmly seated in the industry as a leading editing provider to independent authors and small publishing houses, Hot Tree Publishing is the sister company to Hot Tree Editing, founded in 2012. Having established in-house editing and promotions, plus having a well-respected market presence, Hot Tree Publishing endeavors to be a leader in bringing quality stories to the world of readers.

Interested in discovering more amazing reads brought to you by Hot Tree Publishing or perhaps you're interested in submitting a manuscript and joining the HTPubs family? Either way, head over to the website for information:

WWW.HOTTREEPUBLISHING.COM

CPSIA information can be obtained
at www.ICGtesting.com
Printed in the USA
LVHW111332180820
663514LV00001B/120

9 781925 448221